THE CROWN JEWEL

Drew Logan

The Crown Jewel
Drew Logan
Copyright © 2023
Published by TDLA
TXu002389306

ISBN: 979-8-9896665-7-7

74

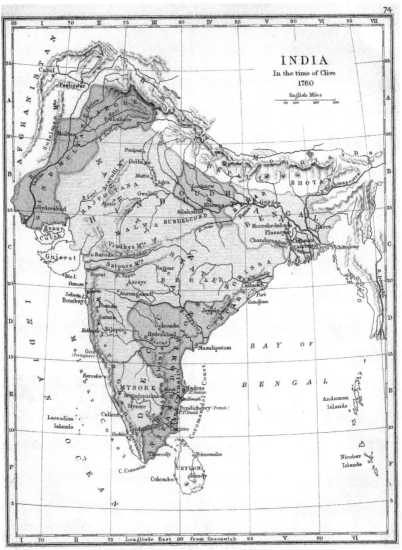

INDIA
In the time of Clive
1760

English Miles

Longmans, Green & Co. London, New York & Bombay.

Inspired by True Events

For My Mother and Father

INTRODUCTION

India, a land so ripe with opportunity, resources, and such breathtaking beauty it wasn't a surprise many came from all over to stake their claim to the Crown Jewel. Among them were the Dutch, French, and Portuguese. However, Great Britain's tenure was by far the most noteworthy as well as the deadliest. Their vehicle into the nation was known as the East India Company (EIC). Originally sent to trade tea, spices, silk, opium, cotton, indigo, and many other things, the EIC eventually turned into a war machine, starting battles and collecting taxes directly from the people of India. Driven by greed, the EIC did whatever it could to expand its territory and enhance its fortune.

At the midpoint of the 18th century, the nation of India was extremely fragmented, more a group of individual nation states and territories than a unified country. The nation consisted of the Mughal and Maratha Empires, whose vast areas covered much of India; other regions and provinces included the Oudh State in the north, Bengal Subah in the east, the Kingdom of Mysore in the South, and the Nizam-controlled Hyderabad state in the central part of the country. The EIC was aware of the disunity among the tribes and used it to their advantage, often times brokering deals with certain rulers and pitting kingdoms and regions against one another.

Indian rulers were granted pseudo power, playing by the rules of the EIC until they could take it no longer. Once this happened they would revolt. Their efforts of rebellion were soon quelled and once again someone else would be placed on a puppet throne by the British. The cycle perpetuated again and again. The names were exchanged, but the results were the same—a weakened local government and a military enterprise exerting firm control over the people of India.

That being said, not all blame should fall on the shoulders of the EIC. Many rulers of the surrounding territories severely hurt their nation by their own self-centered ambitions. They were more interested in getting rich than caring for the needs of the people. Also, many citizens joined the ranks of the EIC, believing they would be better off. These men were known as *sepoys*. At one point, the majority of the EIC's army was made up of sepoys. They fought against their own people and helped Great Britain gain even greater control.

With or without the sepoys, the East India Company was good at what they did and that was to obtain what they wanted, when they wanted it, however they wanted it. The job was never finished. There was always more work to be done, more resources to obtain, and more land to claim. Unfortunately, as profitable as they may have seemed, their ambitious endeavors came with a steep price—a price to be paid by the people of India.

PROLOGUE

June 1756
India

The EIC had been in India for over 150 years already and Siraj ud-Daulah had reached his tipping point. As the newest viceroy of Bengal, officially known as *"Nawab"*, the young ruler had been raised to hate the British. No matter how many treaties were formed with other Indian rulers, the British consistently came out on top. They leveraged every war and negotiation to their advantage. The needs of the Indian people were secondary because it was always about the selfish interests of the East India Company. He couldn't take anymore and decided to launch an attack.

Siraj ud-Daulah led his troops to Calcutta, which was

the heart of British India and would eventually become the capital. Using stealth and a massive amount of manpower, the Nawab invaded Fort William, the EIC's most fortified stronghold in all of India. Originally built in 1696, Fort William was the headquarters of the East India Company and a beacon of British civilization. It was also one of the major entry points into India for the EIC. The British soldiers never saw the attack coming. Knowing they were highly outnumbered, they fled in droves, leaving a few behind who were captured by their enemy. Siraj ud-Daulah was now firmly in charge of Fort William. His generals decided all of the prisoners would be taken to the dungeon known as the Black Hole. The Black Hole was intended for only a few prisoners; however, over five dozen men were forced inside. What happened next was pure pandemonium. Suffocation, claustrophobia, and exhaustion killed over forty people.

The EIC was outraged by what had taken place and immediately decided to retaliate. Robert Clive was chosen to lead the counterattack. Clive, a man known for his eloquence, temper, and most importantly his military prowess was not going to have one of the EIC's most valuable assets snatched away. The loss of Fort William would be detrimental to the company's pocketbooks, not to mention their pride. Knowing they were vastly undermanned, Clive and his soldiers used the element of surprise along with their superior arsenal of weaponry. Siraj ud-Daulah and his army put up somewhat of a resistance, but ultimately it was not enough, and they were defeated. The Bengalis lost Fort William as well as

Calcutta for good.

Unlike Siraj ud-Daulah, not everyone in India minded having the East India Company around, as long as it helped to advance their own personal agendas. One of those individuals who longed to sit on the throne himself was Mir Jafar, commander of the Bengal Army. When Clive heard of the possible mutiny, a deal was proposed. If Mir Jafar and his men aided the EIC against Siraj ud-Daulah, the EIC would be allowed to continue their operation rent free! Not to mention, they would also receive a large sum of money. In return, Clive would make Mir Jafar the next Nawab of Bengal. Mir Jafar gladly agreed. When the day of battle came, Siraj ud-Daulah and his army were easily defeated. Siraj ud-Daulah was executed, and Mir Jafar was installed as the Nawab.

Although it may have looked as if peace had finally been achieved, it didn't last. This conflict, known as the Battle of Plassey, would set the stage for even greater animosity and hostility moving forward between the people of India and the East India Company. Not long after, Mir Jafar became incensed against the EIC, feeling they had become far too powerful. When his betrayal was found out, the EIC replaced him with Mir Qasim. Like his predecessors before him, it would only be a matter of time before Mir Qasim would eventually turn against the EIC. The endless wars would continue and each battle would result in a similar outcome: more power for the East India Company.

With the EIC stronger than ever, Robert Clive returned to England in 1760 a very rich and influential man. Despite the fact that he was gone for a period of time, the show would go on. The EIC would continue its operation, no matter who was at the helm.

Although their task appeared to be impossible, it didn't stop many brave men and women from standing up against the tyranny of the East India Company.

This is one of their tales.

ONE

"There it is, sir!" a young EIC crewmember exclaimed. Through the thickening fog, the flag of England could be seen flying proudly in the sky.

"More coming in, eh? I thought that was the last of em' for a while," a dockworker retorted in a cockney accent.

"Shut up and keep it moving! You bloody well know what you signed up for," Lieutenant Colonel Thomas Webb shouted back at him. Webb turned back to yell at the rest of the men aboard: "Let's go, let's go, let's go! We have two ships waiting to get into the harbor."

In a frenzy, the men scurried around as they unloaded the ship as fast as they could. Carelessly, they tossed wooden chests onto the dock. "Be careful with those!" Webb voraciously screamed. The ire poured out of him like smoke from a chimney. His pointed hat added another two inches to his already gargantuan frame. He looked on as the men scurried around with wheelbarrows. His menacing dark eyes checked the manifest, making sure everything was accounted for. The dockworker nodded his head, muttering under his breath as he headed back into the almost empty ship followed by the younger crewmember.

Webb, second in command at Fort William, had been with the company eight-and-a-half years. He was one of the fortunate ones who had survived the Black Hole and wouldn't let anyone forget it. He also served alongside Robert Clive during the Battle of Plassey, gaining the trust of the most powerful man in the EIC.

After the last of the goods were unloaded, a new ship made its way into the harbor. The men stood at attention, trying to see who or what could be on it. It could be anything from spices, tea, opium, apes, or even humans. With so many ships coming in and going out lately, one never knew what the cargo might be.

Webb looked up to see Clive's replacement, John Carnac, the new Commander in Chief of the EIC walking toward him. Carnac descended onto the dock from the ship and took a long look at his new surroundings.

"General, we were not expecting you until weeks' end. Nevertheless, Fort William is at your service," Webb said as he removed his hat to salute.

"Thomas, you've done well. Word of your ruthless

grip on this place has not only reached Madras but even Parliament. Clive is pleased, and so am I."

Webb couldn't have been happier with the glowing endorsement. Carnac stretched out his bony hand and the old friends embraced. They used to work together in Madras where Carnac had been stationed for the majority of his time in India. General Carnac, twenty years his senior, wasn't quite as tall as Webb but his presence was just as equally intimidating.

"Where are we at with today's shipments?" Carnac asked.

"Evansworth, please give the General an update," Webb replied, looking to his assistant.

"We are a little bit behind schedule, sir." Evansworth nervously stated.

Carnac, annoyed, lit his pipe. "What's specifically heading outbound?" Carnac asked. The smoke blew right into the face of the young assistant.

"Mostly spices, sir," he said, coughing.

"Such as?" Carnac pressed.

"Cardamom, turmeric, cumin… just to name a few, sir."

"Very well."

"It seems like all Her Majesty wants are spices."

"Indeed she does, chap!"

Evansworth beamed.

Carnac continued. "We give them what they want, and they stay off our back."

"That'll be all. Go help the others," Webb barked.

Evansworth's shoulders slumped, and his grin faded as he headed back to the ship.

Carnac took a deep hit from his pipe as crewmembers loaded the docks with barrels. He walked over to one and lifted the lid off; it was filled with rifles. He grabbed one and aimed it at a deckhand, scaring him half to death. He laughed as he put it back into the barrel.

"Spectacular. The new ones are truly a work of art."

"Yes they are, sir."

"Thomas, how pleased are you with the sepoy training?"

"Very pleased. We are finding out that only a few rupees will cause these savages to betray their brothers. In a few years' time, our entire army will be made up of them."

"Excellent, Thomas! Excellent!"

"Yes, sir. Except I must warn you of one thing." Webb paused, searching for the right words.

"Go on."

"Well, sir, it has come to our attention that there are talks of an uprising in several of the villages. We've sent spies out to get a better grasp on the situation."

"That's what we have these for," Carnac said as he patted the barrel of rifles. "Very good though. We can never be too comfortable. It can't be anything compared to what we've already been through with Siraj ud-Daulah."

"I hope not, but I don't want to take any chances. One loss of English life isn't worth fifty brown men."

"Ah, you see that's where you have it wrong. Not all English are the same." Carnac pointed to an overweight sailor who was having a hard time getting his load of cargo up the steep ramp. "I'll trade his fat arse for five dead Indians right now."

Webb started to scream at the large man, but Carnac raised his hand to stop him. "Don't waste your energy, Thomas," he said, "we need every man we can get. The barbarians far outnumber us."

"Numbers are the only thing they have on us."

"The good thing for us is they aren't organized. Clive always said it would be their downfall."

"If they just banded together as one, they would destroy us," Webb whispered.

"But they never will. You see, in this jungle, it's every bloke for himself, you've seen it firsthand with the sepoys. Why are they fighting for us in the first place?"

"Because they are selfish, sir?"

"It's more than that. Every mate is selfish. It's called pride. These people fight in their bare feet with sticks. We, on the other hand, are civilized. How do you think they feel when they see us with our polished boots and war medals, not to mention our stockpile of munitions?"

"I don't know, sir."

"Of course, you do. You felt it the moment you landed in Madras years ago. You remember what it felt like to put on the uniform. You know how the lassies talked about you and still do. Everybody wants to be a part of something bigger than themselves. The Company gave us that opportunity, and now we are giving it to them. The sepoys realize we are the future. We are doing these people a favor."

With that final statement, General Carnac walked over to a sepoy whose chest had just fallen off his wheelbarrow. Among its contents now littered on the

13

ground was a spool of black silk beginning to unravel. The man quivered as he tried as quickly as he could to get the spool back in alignment.

"Don't you worry about that. You just keep up the good work," Carnac said as he put his hand on the man's shoulder, eliciting a rare smile. Carnac helped the sepoy put the rest of the loose items back into the chest.

"Come! Let's go up to the office. I've heard about Clive's opium stash. I want to get my hands on some of it."

"Right this way, sir," Webb snickered.

The two men walked toward the gates of Fort William and disappeared inside.

TWO

Burdwan
68 miles northeast of Fort William

"**W**hy does mine look so different than yours?" Annie Door asked in a playful tone as she held up a red scarf she had been knitting. "It's so much smaller!" A few women nearby whispered in Bengali and began laughing. She was quickly shown where she went wrong.

"Oh! You have to go over and then under? I was doing it backwards. I'll get the hang of this. Just wait and see." The women giggled again. Everyone loved Annie. She was funny, smart, and could handle living in a part of the world where most westerners wouldn't dream of going. Annie looked over her shoulder to check on her only child, Colt, who was playing cricket with the other kids of the village.

"Let's go, Rafa! Quit stalling!" The thirteen-year-old yelled as he twirled a wooden bat. The ball came through and *whack!* Colt sent it sailing. The other boys chased after it only to be outrun by Zara, Rafa's younger sister. She tossed the ball back to her brother. Although several of the villagers knew English, Rafa and Zara were the only kids who could speak it. Their father, Pradeep, a wealthy landowner, made sure his kids learned the language at a young age.

"My turn!" she exclaimed.

"No!" Rafa fired back. "Boys only!"

"You said, 'whoever gets to the ball first gets to bat next.'"

"She's right, you did say that," Colt said as he handed her the bat.

"Fine! But you only get one swing," Rafa angrily replied.

Zara stepped up in front of the wicket. Rafa wound up and threw the ball as hard as he could throw it. Zara swung and didn't even come close. The other kids started to laugh.

"Next!" Rafa bellowed.

"Come on man, no one could have hit that," Colt said, coming to Zara's defense.

"Too bad, I said one swing. Go knit with mom."

Tears started to well in Zara's eyes, and she dropped the bat.

"Why do you have to be like that?" Colt asked,

annoyed.

"If she wants to run with the big boys, she's got to learn to bat like one. Who's up next?" Another boy picked up the bat hastily as Zara ran away.

Not far from where the boys were playing, a group of men stood around talking to Colt's father, John Door. John was a protestant missionary and carpenter by trade from the colony of Pennsylvania. He was also the only white man they could trust, and he had proved that time and time again. John often offered his wood working expertise and helped with many building projects in the community, never charging for his services.

The men formed a circle around him as they vented to him about their distrust of the EIC. All sorts of men of various occupations stood before him: farmers, shepherds, smiths, and different types of tradesmen. Some had on the finest silk while others were covered with dirt from the fields. John had listened to their individual complaints for weeks now. However, he had never witnessed anything like this. Their emotions boiled over and now their voices were coming at him from all directions.

"They took everything. My father had sixty acres. I don't even have ten now!" a farmer complained.

"Me too! Only now I have nothing," another chimed in.

"More and more surveyors are showing up unannounced," a large property owner exclaimed as he clapped his hands in anger.

"We have to get our land back!" another voice proclaimed.

17

"Qasim is raising an army. I will go and fight tomorrow. I'd rather die than live like this!" a blacksmith screamed.

The men cheered in agreement. As the shouting ensued, another man named Dari slipped into the back of the crowd. John lifted up his hand, indicating he would like to say something. A hush fell over the men as they anxiously awaited his words.

"We must be careful. We cannot afford to have another repeat of Plassey." John said calmly.

"We have to do something," a silk trader murmured.

"I agree. But if we attack right away, it will only make things worse," John answered him.

"I say we fight today!" The farmer lifted his pitchfork in the air, causing the men to shout in unison.

"Do you want to give up more land?" John cried out. "Do you want to pay higher taxes? Do you want your wives and children to become their slaves? Because that's what you are asking for."

There was no response to his words as tension filled the air.

Finally, a humble woodworker spoke up. "What do you suppose we do? You've seen what they have taken already. It's just a matter of time before their entire army comes here."

All eyes turned to John as they waited for his reply. He looked over at Colt who was deeply engaged in an intense game of cricket. His eyes then fell upon Annie who was laughing as she untangled a knot. His heart began to pound as his eyes focused on the faces that surrounded him. The words he desperately didn't want to say finally came from his mouth.

"I will go to Patna."

"What? No! This isn't your fight," Pradeep said.

John continued and his voice grew stronger with each syllable. "I will go to Patna, and I will talk to the company officials. Something has to change."

He took another quick glance at Colt who was clearly enjoying himself for the first time in a long time.

"We will go with you," Pradeep promptly added.

"Thank you my dear friend, but you know I must go alone. Anything else will look suspicious."

"What makes you think anything will change?" Dari said sarcastically from the back of the crowd.

"Unlike the ones at Fort William, I have heard there are men in Patna with open minds," John replied.

"Why are you helping us?" the woodworker asked.

"Because it's the right thing to do. The fight against tyranny is everyone's fight. My people are fighting the same battle on the other side of the world."

"What should we do in the meantime?" the blacksmith inquired.

"Unite the tribes. Send word to the Marathas and the Mysoreans, we must get them to join the Mughals and Qasim's army. We can't wage any more separate wars."

Dari spoke up again, discouraging the idea. "But everyone hates each other. There's no way that would ever happen."

"We don't have a choice; they are too strong," John countered. "For the time being, stop trading with the EIC."

"If we stop trading, how will I support my family?" a merchant asked.

"Trade with the Dutch or the French, anyone but the British. We must dry up their supply chain. We have to hit them where it hurts."

The men nodded their heads in agreement.

"Just please do me one favor—watch over my wife and son."

"John, after everything you've done for us, you know we will." Pradeep said as he gave him a hug. The rest of the men clapped John on the back, and he tipped his hat in gratitude. He turned to go and made his way through the crowd.

"Mr. Door, do you really think you can take down the EIC?" Dari mocked once more.

John took a long, hard look at him and then at the rest of the men gathered around him.

"If the people of India come together, the EIC doesn't stand a chance!"

Loud roars erupted from the men of Burdwan while Dari's face turned sour. As the men continued to cheer enthusiastically, Dari slowly snuck away unnoticed. He jumped on a horse tethered to a nearby tree and headed in the direction of Fort William.

THREE

The Doors' cabin had been built by the previous owner, another missionary. It was pretty bare when they moved in; however, Annie had made the house into a home. Fresh flowers were always on the table. Marigolds and poppies were her favorites. An old stove was in the corner used for cooking meals and drying out clothes. It was rarely, if ever, used to heat the house. In northeast India, keeping warm was not something one generally needed to worry about. Colt enjoyed seeing the stove. It reminded him of his grandparents' place back in America. The transition had been hard for him, but he was doing the best he could do.

"Dad, you should have seen me today! I did so good!" Colt said as he whizzed around the kitchen, swinging an imaginary bat in the air.

"I did see you! You played awesome!"

"Everybody likes to watch me bat because I can hit it so far! I kind of felt bad because they kept chasing after the ball."

"Did you let the other kids have a turn?" Annie asked as she stirred a pot, sending out an earthy aroma into the room.

"Of course, I did, Mom . . . hey, what is that?" Colt asked inquisitively as he peered into a bowl of onions, rice, ghee, and an assortment of other things he didn't recognize all mixed together.

"I'm making a new dish called *Mutton Biryani*. I guess it's a traditional thing, one of the ladies gave me the recipe. I love those gals; they've been so welcoming and kind to me."

The people of Burdwan had gone above and beyond for the Doors. They constantly showered them with gifts, especially saris for Annie. She wore a different color every single day, while the rest were kept in a teak chest in her bedroom John made for her when they first moved to India.

"It looks good," John added as he leaned over and kissed his wife.

"That's gross!" Colt exclaimed as he turned away quickly.

"Go wash up for dinner, sweetie. Dinner is almost ready."

Colt took one more giant swing with his fictitious bat before he scampered out of the room. John leaned in and gave Annie another kiss. This time, it was longer than usual.

"John, what is it that you want to tell me?"

"Am I that predictable?"

"After being married for close to twenty years, I would say yes," she added with a suspicious smile, unsure of what he was about to say. John gazed deeply into her blue eyes as he chose his words carefully.

"Do you remember what I specifically said to you before I asked you to move here last year?"

Fighting the pit that had begun to form in her stomach, she recited the events of the day verbatim. She remembered the moment as if it were yesterday.

"We were at your father's. It started raining really hard and we ran onto to the porch. I was soaked, and I wanted to go inside to get warm. But you stopped me just before I could go in. You said, 'Will you trust me?' And now, here we are. How could I forget it?"

John wrapped his arms around her and whispered in her ear. "You know I love you and Colt more than anything in this world."

"I know," the pit was fully formed now.

"I'm going to ask you the same thing again one more time."

"You already know the answer to that," she quietly responded as her eyes moistened. Colt appeared back inside of the kitchen.

"Is everything okay?"

"Yes, sweetheart," Annie added as she dried her eyes with her apron. She turned her attention back to the biryani. "Let's eat. Colt, dear, will you set the table?"

No one said anything as Colt got out the plates. Annie's mind raced as they ate in silence. Finally, after a few minutes, John spoke up.

"Day after tomorrow, I am going to Patna. The EIC's power has gotten completely out of control. They are wreaking havoc among the people."

Colt slammed down his fork causing his water to spill onto the table. "Dad, are you kidding? Why?"

"Son, someone has got to stand up to them. What they are doing is horribly wrong. These people really need our help."

"I don't understand why this concerns you! You aren't even Indian or British!"

"Skin color has nothing to do with it. The right thing to do is the right thing to do."

"But it's not our war!" Colt raged.

"Colt, don't speak to your father like that," Annie said sternly.

"And you are just going to let him go?"

Annie didn't respond.

"Of course you are. I never wanted to come here in the first place!" Colt bolted from the table in an uproar and headed for the door.

"Colt, get back here now!" Annie demanded.

"Annie, let him go," John said softly.

Colt slammed the door shut, causing the entire house to shake. He sobbed as he made his way onto Pradeep's land, finding a hiding place in one of the fields. He wasn't by himself long. Zara, who had spotted him running across her yard, slowly approached him. When he saw her, he buried his tear-stained face into her shoulder.

Meanwhile, back at the cabin, John and Annie continued their discussion.

"John, I've never seen him so upset."

"That's been bottled up inside him for a while."

"I'm going to go get him." She said as she stood up.

"Let him be. He needs his space right now."

"Do you really think you are going to be able to make a difference?" She said, sitting back down.

"I have to try. I can't sit back and watch this country get swallowed up by injustice."

"What are you going to do?"

"I'm just going to talk with the company officials to see if something can be worked out. There has to be someone within reach of the Crown. I don't believe everyone in London would be on board with what they are doing here."

Annie nodded her head in agreement as John continued, "Do you realize at this very moment, Mir Qasim is raising an army against the EIC? The worst part is there's no unity among the tribes and they know that. If we don't do something, another war will ensue, and more lives will be lost. And I can't live with that. The people of this country mean too much to me."

"I guess I'm just scared." Annie stared at her plate, still untouched.

"I am too." He said, visibly upset.

Annie had never heard John admit that he was scared

before. Gaining strength from deep within her, she rose from the table again. "My parents said we were crazy for moving here," she said as she drew near to him. "but deep down I knew we had too. 'Walk by faith, not by sight,' right?"

John smiled and took her hand.

Annie continued. "We didn't know what to expect. But looking back now, when I think about how much I love these people, I wouldn't change anything. So, when you tell me that you have to do this, I won't stand in your way."

"You know what this could mean?"

"Well, we just can't think about that right now." Annie slowly wiped a tear away from John's eye. "Go check on Colt."

He kissed her and walked outside.

FOUR

Knowing Colt would be somewhere on Pradeep's farm, he headed in that direction. He walked along the dusty road and observed the different houses and the fires burning within. Sounds of laughter and barking dogs filled the streets. Each place he passed by conjured up a happy memory. He recalled the many conversations he had around the warm hearths. The cool evening breeze was a friendly feeling on John's tired face. Today had been a hard day and it took a sudden turn. One minute he was sharing his faith with a few men, and the next he had told the entire village he would be heading to Patna to take on the East India Company. It was one thing to stand in front of a cheering crowd, and another to now walk alone. Faith fought doubt, as the voices inside his head waged war against each other.

He paused for a moment as he approached Pradeep's

plantation. This was the first place he and Annie had stayed in Burdwan. Memories of those first few nights came flooding back.

If you don't, who will?

John stopped in his tracks. Although he hadn't heard it in a while, he knew that voice all too well. He gazed at the twinkling stars and was reminded why he had come to India in the first place. Hope soared within his soul.

As he made his way onto the property, he could see through the moonlight that Colt wasn't alone. Zara was sitting next to him. She jumped up when she saw John.

"Hello, Zara."

"Hi, Mr. Door."

"Thanks for keeping him company."

Zara blushed and headed back to her house. Colt didn't want Zara to go. He liked being around her. John sat down next to him in a field of barley and the two of them watched the crops dance back and forth in the gentle wind.

Breaking the silence between them, John said, "I can see why you like to come here. It kind of reminds me of Grandpa's."

Colt, not ready to say anything, stared up at the rising moon.

"I'm sorry I sprung that on you like that. I should have talked to you before I made a final decision."

Colt shrugged his shoulders.

"I don't know if I ever told you about my Grandpa Lloyd."

Colt finally spoke up. "All I know is that he came over

28

from England and that's how we got the farm."

"That's right. But I want to tell you why he left when everyone around him told him not to."

Colt was interested now. He had never heard this part of the story. He sat up as his father continued talking.

"For starters he was an older man. He had a successful business and a beautiful estate in Essex. He was wealthy and lived a very comfortable life. He could buy anything a man could want. But he felt something was missing and didn't know what that was until he met a group of people called the Quakers."

"The Quakers? Why were they called the Quakers?"

"There are several theories. One being that when they were in worship, they would start to quake because their experience was so powerful."

"I don't know about that. That seems kinda weird to me," Colt said suspiciously.

"It would definitely be odd to someone who didn't understand. But what if you were the one having the undeniable experience?"

Colt pondered at his words, not thinking anything like that was even possible. "Has anything like that ever happened to you?"

"I have certainly had experiences that were unexplainable, and I realized I was in the presence of someone much more powerful than myself," John carefully responded.

Colt, unsure of what to think, looked up at his dad. "So, what ended up happening to him?"

"Well, when he was around the Quakers, he could

see there was something different about them. When he found out what it was, it changed his life forever. He was impacted by his newfound faith so much that when a group of them moved to America to get away from the oppression of England, he sold everything and went with them."

"Is that why we came to India?"

"Yes, something like that. I told you that story because I wanted you to know why I do what I do. I wouldn't do something like this if I didn't believe I was supposed to. You may not understand now, but I hope one day you will." John stood up, "Come on, Tiger, let's go see Mom."

FIVE

The day for John's departure had arrived. Colt was still upset by his father's decision to leave, but he knew there was nothing he could do about it. Even if he tried to talk him out of it, he couldn't change his father's mind. John believed with all his heart that he was supposed to go, and somehow his mom believed that as well.

A group of villagers had just left the cabin, including Pradeep, his wife Bindu, Rafa, and Zara. The people of Burdwan showered the Doors with gifts and well wishes, leaving John and Annie encouraged. The people were behind them and appreciated everything the Doors had done for them.

When John was to return from his trip, he planned on having a discussion with the heads of the different tribes and territories with hopes of forming an alliance. He knew if they remained isolated, it would be just a matter of time before they all were defeated at the hands of the EIC. But he believed if they were to unite, they would stand victorious. He really looked forward to trying to bring the Marathas and Mysoreans together. As improbable as it may have seemed, he believed the common foe of the EIC could unite even the fiercest of enemies. Word had been sent by the village elders to the four corners of the country. Now they waited with anticipation that everyone would gather before Mir Qasim—or anyone else—decided to unleash a solo attack.

Pradeep offered John one of his finest Marwari horses to take to Patna. The breed descended from the mighty Rajput warhorses. John brushed the big black horse affectionately known as Motu. A deep peace came over him. Even though the trip he was about to embark on was extremely dangerous, he had to go. He constantly reminded Colt: "The hardest thing to do was usually the right thing to do." Now it was his opportunity to put those words into practice.

"Are you sure you have everything?" Annie asked as she handed him warm bread.

"I think so. Thanks, honey." John double checked his leather satchel and tightened the bed roll behind the saddle.

Colt emerged from the house with a few slices of mango for Motu, who gobbled them up from his hand. He pushed down the feelings of sorrow that had risen up ever since he heard the news his father would be leaving. Motu nuzzled his head against Colt's neck; the horse clearly enjoyed his company.

"He likes you. Pradeep said he isn't fond of many people."

"It's just because I gave him food."

"I gave him some earlier and he didn't warm up to me that quickly."

John got down on his knees and looked up at his beloved son. "As I've told you time and time again, you are special, Colt. Don't ever forget that. You will be used to accomplish great things."

Motu broke up the moment and licked the side of Colt's face, which caused both of them to laugh. "I told you. Animals can sense that sort of thing."

"I love you, son."

"I love you too, Dad."

John wiped away a tear making its way down Colt's cheek. "Take care of your mother."

"I will," Colt said quietly as he gave his dad one final hug.

John stood and wrapped his arms around his wife, kissing her passionately. He got onto the majestic creature, settling himself in the saddle. He put his hat on and waved goodbye to the lingering villagers. The horse trotted northwest as Colt and Annie's figures faded into the distance.

SIX

One week later
Fort William

General Carnac's boots rested on the mahogany desk amidst other papers and letters from England. The large desk was located in the upper room that served as the Commander in Chief's headquarters. It overlooked the entire courtyard of the fort. Since Fort William was a revolving door, many leaders of the EIC claimed the room as their own. For the time being, it belonged to Carnac. He knew he should enjoy this brief moment of power because it wouldn't last long, seeing that at any moment's notice, Clive would return. There was no question he appreciated and secretly admired all Clive had done for the EIC. But whenever he wanted to get ahead, it seemed

Clive was right in front of him. Clive was their "golden boy" and quite frankly, he was the second choice and always would be. Lost in introspection, he heard a knock at the door.

"Come in," Carnac said, not leaving the desk.

Dari entered the room alongside Webb. "Sir, this is the sepoy I was telling you about. He's just arrived from Burdwan."

"What do you have for me?"

"Sahib, I have something big, but I need guarantees," Dari said confidently.

"Please, do you know who you are speaking to? When we are in complete control, you will be living like the Nawab."

"Okay. About nine months ago, a missionary named John Door and his wife came to Burdwan from America."

"Why was I not informed?" Thomas Webb immediately jumped in.

"I did not think it was relevant. Missionaries travel to all parts of the world, including here," Dari retorted.

"I determine what's relevant and what is not!" Webb snapped back as he poked Dari in the chest.

"Relax, Thomas," Carnac replied, reasserting control over the room. "What about this man? Please continue."

"He has been meeting with the men of our village and sharing with them from a holy book, which he always does. But recently the topics of the meetings have changed.

"In what way?" Carnac asked, not amused.

"Things began to get, shall I say, more political."

35

With that statement, Dari grinned like a Cheshire cat. He had their full attention now. "I normally do not stay for the meetings, but when the change occurred, I knew I couldn't miss it. The men were complaining about the EIC." He paused, relishing in the moment, never in his life had he felt this important. He continued, his voice growing louder by the second "and then with my own ears, I heard this man encourage a rebellion. He advised the people to unite the tribes if they wanted a chance at defeating your army. He also recommended they stop trading with you and to start trading with the Dutch and French."

"He what?" General Carnac said as he jerked his legs off his desk, sending a stack of papers flying to the floor.

"But that is not all, Sahib. He spoke of traveling to Patna to have some kind of peace talks with the officials there."

Aware of his outburst, General Carnac straightened his jacket and regained his composure. "And when is this going to take place?"

"Very soon."

"You have outdone yourself, sepoy."

Carnac took out a bag of coins from the desk and tossed them to Dari.

Webb spoke up. "General, send him straight to Qasim. We need to nip this in the bud. We cannot afford another incident like the Black Hole."

"Thomas, that is brilliant. Sepoy, come here. There is one more thing I want you to do."

"Anything Sahib."

36

"Go to Qasim and tell him that this John Door is one of us. Tell him that the American missionary has persuaded the majority of the outlying villages to sell their land to the EIC and that he is going to go to Patna to receive further instruction."

"Yes sir. I will head there now."

"Good boy. Good dogs get extra treats." Carnac threw Dari a few more coins. The coins clanked on the ground. Dari clamored on all fours, picking them up as quickly as he could.

SEVEN

Colt adjusted to his father being gone by spending every free moment he had with Rafa and Zara—that was, whenever Rafa allowed Zara to tag along. Usually, Colt had a specific time he had to be home at night, but since his father had left, his mother had flexed the rules. Knowing her son was having a hard time, she hoped the freedom would cheer him up. When Colt wasn't being home-schooled, he spent the majority of his time exploring the outskirts of the village or playing cricket.

"That's it. I'm beat," Rafa said as he dropped to the ground after an intense game.

"Oh, come on, I'm just getting warmed up!" Colt bounced the ball on the end of the bat as he tried to see how many times he could keep it going without it falling.

Rafa peeled a banana that his mom had given him, "What was America like?"

Taken aback, Colt stopped and sat down next to him. "Totally different from here."

"How?"

"Well, it's not this hot and it doesn't rain as much," Colt said, giggling.

"Yeah, it is pretty hot here and it definitely rains a lot. What did your family do back there?"

"We had a big farm, kind of like your dad's, only we didn't have horses."

"You didn't have horses? Why?"

"I don't know."

"My dad said when I get older I can have Motu."

"Your dad let my dad take Motu on his trip."

Rafa could tell that Colt was sad and tried to cheer him up. "Well, I'm glad you are here, and I know Zara is too."

Colt quickly changed the conversation, as he felt his face getting red. "There's one thing I don't like about America."

"What's that?"

"We don't have cricket."

"I don't think I could live there then." Rafa said as he sat up. "Okay, I'm ready to play now." Rafa handed Colt the bat. "Let's see if you can hit my fastball."

"Now that's easy."

The two boys started laughing.

Annie was also having a tough time since John left. The ladies of the village were extremely kind and routinely made meals for her. But she didn't really have anyone to talk too. No one understood what she was actually going through. This was the first time in nearly twenty years she had been separated from her husband. She found herself writing in her diary more than she ever had before. One night while Colt was out, she wrote about how difficult her day had been. Then out of nowhere, as if something had taken over her, she wrote these words: *It's not about me*. Unsure of why she would write something like that, she scribbled out the words and continued to pour her heart out on the page. She shared how lonely she felt, only to subconsciously find herself writing that little phrase again. *It's not about me*. Stunned, she looked down at what she had just written and meditated on the phrase.

Annie believed in the power of words and understood things like that don't just happen.

"Who talks like that?" she mused.

Then her gaze slowly fell on the old book on the nightstand beside the bed.

"That's who."

Her mind shifted back to John. He was so quick to put others first. That's one of the things she admired most about him. Annie opened the timeless book and flipped through the pages, finding a verse recently circled: *Where I am going, you cannot follow Me now, but you shall follow Me afterward*. The verse sent chills down her spine and she slammed the book shut. She tried to tell herself it was just a mere coincidence, but she knew better. The pit in her stomach returned in full force.

⁓

Dari walked past the armed guards with their sleek turbans wrapped around their heads and was ushered into the inner court of Mir Qasim. He quietly whispered into the Nawab's ear. Upon hearing the words, Qasim angrily jumped to his feet.

"It is time!" he shouted.

EIGHT

The door creaked open, and Colt slowly snuck into the house. He assumed his mom was asleep. He tiptoed around the kitchen, trying to be as quiet as he could. The attempt was unsuccessful. He didn't see the handle of the cast-iron skillet sticking out from the stove. He ran right into it. It crashed to the ground, sending a loud sound throughout the house.

"Colt! What in the world?" Annie said as she hurried into the kitchen with a candle. Chicken curry was all over the floor.

"I'm sorry, Mom. I didn't even see it." Together they cleaned up the mess and sat down at the table. The candle flickered, looking as if it were ready to go out at any moment.

"Have you heard anything?"

"Not yet, but I am sure he is there by now. Colt, I

42

want to show you something." Annie left the room and returned with a letter clutched in her hands. Colt had never seen it before. As she sat back down at the table and looked into his eyes, the pit in her stomach dissolved. "There's something I've been meaning to share with you." Her smile met his confused face. "The day after you were born, I had the same dream three days in a row. I was carrying you, and we were walking through a remote village somewhere in India. I heard a noise and walked over to see what it was. Behind a thatched door was a mother crying over her kids who were starving to death. I didn't know what to do. So, I just walked up to her and let her hold you. As soon as I did that she stopped crying."

"What happened after that?" Colt asked curiously.

"That was it. I told your father about it, and we both felt it was significant—but neither of us knew what to do. Then thirteen years later, we got this in the mail." Annie held up the letter and she began to read aloud.

John,
Hope this letter finds you and Annie well. I
will make this brief. I wanted to inform you
of some big news. I have accepted a position at
St. John's church in Tiruchirappalli. Everyone
just calls it Trichy though. We are hoping
to start a school soon. My parents were not
pleased with my decision to leave London.
However, I knew it was the right thing to do.
India is where I am called to be. I also wanted

*to inform you that Wesley Stullman has left
his post in Burdwan. When asked about a
possible replacement, your name came up.
Please give this invitation some serious prayer
and consideration. I think it would be the
perfect fit.*

*I cannot wait until I see your faces and
finally get to meet Colt!*
In His name,
Peter

Her voice cracked as she barely made out the last couple
of words. "We left a month later."

"So, we just moved halfway across the world because
of a dream and a letter?"

"I would like to think there was more to it than that."

"What else was there?"

"Faith is hard to explain because I do not fully
understand it myself. All I can say is your father and I
both knew this was what we were supposed to do."

"That just makes no sense to me," Colt quipped as he
left the table.

"Someday it will."

"I'm gonna call it a night." Colt went to his room and
climbed into bed. He finally fell asleep, tormented by
dreams of Indian mothers weeping and not being able
to do anything to stop it.

The following day, menacing clouds appeared in the
northwest sky. Large droplets of rain fell to the ground
and an unusual humidity rose in the air. The winds

kicked up. The farmers could tell something was wrong. Normally, the rain brought respite from the scorching heat. However, today something was different—very different. They packed up their things and headed for cover.

Annie spotted a funnel cloud in the sky and pointed it out to the other women who quickly called for the children who were playing nearby. Monsoon rains were common in northeast India, but the people of Burdwan had never experienced anything like this.

Fortunately, the funnel cloud passed over the heart of the village, but it wrecked everything else in its path, including several fields. The storm would turn out to be an ominous sign of things to come.

NINE

October

The extreme heat slowly faded away, and the cooler temperatures were greatly welcomed. All over the nation, people prepared for the upcoming celebration of Diwali, the festival of lights. The annual party would last for several days. There would be fireworks, gifts given, feasting, and a lot of sweet things would be eaten.

"Rafa, would you hand me a diya?" Bindu asked. Colt watched Rafa give his mother a small oil lamp that would be used for the holiday. She placed the diya next to a circular piece of artwork. The flickering wick caused the colors to come to life. It was in the shape of a rose made with actual orange and white rose petals.

"What is this?" Colt asked, astounded by the

exquisite flower.

"It's a rangoli. Zara finished it this morning." Bindu replied.

"You did this?" Colt enquired. He glanced at Zara. "It's amazing!" Her cheeks grew bright red and she smiled shyly. Their eyes met and he looked away. Realizing he sounded a bit too excited about the rangoli and wanting to change the subject, he turned to Bindu. "How did Diwali start anyways?"

"Legend has it," her voice grew with animation, "the demon king Ravana kidnapped a beautiful princess named Sita. Her husband, the Great Prince Rama defeated him and rescued his bride. When Rama and Sita finally came back to their kingdom, they found that the entire city was decorated with diyas and flowers, as the people celebrated their return. We carry on the tradition to this very day." Bindu looked directly at Colt and smiled. "Diwali reminds us that ultimately, good will triumph over evil. That brings us hope no matter what obstacles may currently be in our way."

⌒⟶꜆

The day before the holiday officially began, a section of British soldiers rode through Burdwan. Their arrival caused the villagers to panic. Leaving Colt to work on his studies, Annie went outside to see what all the commotion was about. As soon as she left, Colt poked his head outside

47

as he stared at the sea of red uniforms that was now on his quiet street. He listened as his mother spoke to a young officer amidst the crowd that had gathered.

"Can we help you?"

"Yes, ma'am, I am looking for…" He double checked to make sure that he had the correct name. "Annie Door."

"That's me. What can I do for you?"

The officer dismounted his horse and removed his hat as he looked somberly at her.

"What's this about?"

"Ma'am, I am so sorry to be the one to tell you this. We have just come from Patna. It's your husband."

"What about him?"

He hesitated as he struggled to find the words. "Something terrible has happened."

Annie grabbed his jacket. "Tell me *exactly* what happened."

"Mir Qasim's men went on a killing spree. They took the lives of close to fifty individuals. Your husband was one of them." He handed her John's leather bag. "We found this."

Annie stared blankly at him.

The officer lowered his voice and whispered into her ear. "They will be coming for you next. You are not safe here."

"Thank you, sir," she could barely get the words out.

He got back onto his horse, and the soldiers rode away. Annie dropped to her knees as several women of the village wrapped their arms around her. Colt took off, leaving everyone behind. Annie saw him and yelled for him, but he paid no attention and continued to run, faster and faster.

There was no stopping Colt. He had to get away. He wanted to be anywhere but here. Passing by huts and open fields, he sprinted until his legs gave out. He had never been this far from the village and finally stopped in front of a pond surrounded by jackfruit and guava trees. He wept until he could cry no more. It was a beautiful place, but he didn't notice the beauty. Nothing seemed to matter anymore.

Something died inside of Colt that day. The bright-eyed cheerful boy no longer existed, his kind and caring heart was now calloused and cold. He had been perfectly content to remain on his grandfather's land in Pennsylvania. He never wanted to leave that piece of ground to begin with. When he was told they would be leaving for India, he wasn't given the option to stay. He hadn't asked for this. Yet somehow, he had been sucked right into the middle of a war. If they never had left America, none of this would have happened. He hated what his father stood for. His "faith" had gotten him killed. He had already been on the fence with the whole spirituality issue. But when he saw firsthand what could happen to someone who believed in something they couldn't see, the decision had been made firmly in his heart—never again.

Thoughts of his mother came to his mind. She must be so worried about him. As much as he was hurting and wanted to be alone, he wanted to be there for her. He forced himself to walk back to the village.

Annie had already started to pack when Colt walked through the door. Dropping everything, she wrapped her arms around her son.

"I'm sorry, Mom. I just . . ." Colt stammered, unable to get the words out.

"It's okay," Annie interrupted him. "We will get through this. We have to trust the bigger plan."

Colt did everything he could to bite his tongue and not respond to what he heard her say. All his life, he had heard about "the bigger plan," and he was sick of it. But getting in an argument right now was the last thing he wanted. If his mom needed to believe in "the bigger plan," then he wouldn't take that away from her.

"Where are we going?"

"We are going to Trichy to see Peter. We aren't safe here anymore."

"But what about Rafa and Zara?"

"They should be okay."

"Mom, I don't understand."

Annie stopped and brushed the hair away from his eyes, studying his face, not knowing what to say. Somehow, he looked older to her.

"I don't either," she said, finally, as they held onto each other. "Go pack your things. Only take what you can carry."

Colt surveyed his room. He considered taking the stuffed tiger he received when he was an infant, but left it on the bed. He didn't need it, he wasn't a kid anymore. He looked up at his dresser. The miniature soldiers stood at attention, taunting him with their painted faces and bayonets ready for war. He threw one across the room. It fell to the ground in a dozen pieces.

He stepped over the broken pieces of the soldier and came across a stack of books. He remembered how his dad used to read to him. Milton, Chaucer, Shakespeare. He loved hearing his dad imitate the different characters in each story. As he sifted through the pile, he saw *Pilgrim's Progress* lying there as well. This was the next book they were going to read together. He didn't know the story but knew it was one of his dad's favorites. The leather-bound book felt soft and familiar in his hands. He decided to take it with him. After grabbing some clothes he made his way back into the kitchen where he saw his father's old satchel sitting on the table. He traced his fingers across the faded leather.

"Colt, are you almost . . ." Annie stopped midsentence when she saw what he was doing. She quietly headed back into the other room. Colt didn't hear her because he was too busy looking over his dad's old things. A wool sweater, compass, Bible, and maps now lay out on the table in front of him. Assessing what he might need, he stuffed everything except the Bible back into the satchel along with the items from his room.

TEN

The horse-drawn carriage waited outside of the Doors' cabin. Pradeep had arranged for his personal driver to take Annie and John to Calcutta. From there, they would take a ship south to Madras and eventually make their way west to Trichy. The men and women of Burdwan gathered around to pay their condolences. No one had made such a huge impact on the village in such a short amount of time. It seemed as if everyone was there. Annie and Colt were completely blown away by the send-off. Annie hugged those around her as Colt trailed behind. He tried to fight off the emotion and was successful until he heard a familiar voice.

"I am going to miss you, brother." Rafa said as he came alongside him. His best friend placed a cricket ball in his hand. Colt couldn't hold it in any longer and broke down. The tears streamed down his face. As much as he hated being in India, he had never had a friend like Rafa. As Colt turned toward the carriage, he could hear another voice calling to him.

"Colt, wait!" Zara cried out as she made her way through the crowd, not caring what anyone thought.

"Zara!" Colt exclaimed as the tears continued to pour out. They embraced and he held on for as long as he could. He didn't want to let go, being with her had helped soothe the pain of being away from his father. Now he was forced to say goodbye. The grief was almost too much to bear.

"I wish we had more time." Colt whispered in her ear before he pulled away. He climbed up and sat down next to his mother.

"I do too," she said under her breath, as a lone tear slid down her cheek. The driver snapped the reins, and the horses took off.

ELEVEN

Fort William

Colt noticed the changes to the city right away. Calcutta was bustling. This was no doubt due to the EIC's economic expansion. The tents of local merchants had been replaced with British storefronts selling soap, tea, and a variety of other luxuries that would be available to any resident of London. Private clubs and saloons had also been introduced. However, one of the greatest changes were the additions done to Fort William. It was almost unrecognizable.

Standing out like a sore thumb, its majestic entrance served as a monument to Great Britain's ironclad supremacy over the region, warning all to stay out of their way. Colt had seen Fort William once when he first arrived in India. However, that was from a distance, seeing it so closely today made the hair on the back of his neck stand straight up. Maybe it was because of the influx of soldiers or because of the thousands of sepoys being trained to fight in the open fields once used for farming. But most of all, the fear came from being in such a place without his father. But his dad was gone and there was nothing he could do to bring him back.

As they got close to the edge of the harbor, their carriage driver dropped them off. Seeing the water brought some reprieve. The Hooghly River promised a new beginning. Annie had hoped they could catch a boat heading south without being noticed. Colt double-checked his satchel to make sure everything was secure. When he did, he found the Bible had made its way back in. Obviously, his mother had put it in there. He chose not to bring it up.

"We'll catch a ship down there," Annie said, pointing toward the end of a large dock. They briskly marched down the wooden platform, passing by carts of goods soon to be sold at the market. They were only able to get about twenty-five yards when they were stopped by a group of EIC soldiers.

"Right on schedule," a lieutenant said looking at his pocket-watch. "We were told you would be heading this way."

"How can we help you?" Annie responded.

"Ever since the attack last week, we have been keeping a close eye on who comes in and out of the harbor."

"Well, I can assure you we had nothing to do with that."

"The jury is still out on that one, ma'am."

"Excuse me?"

"I am not going to get into it. We will let General Carnac deal with it. Come with us." As Annie protested, four soldiers grabbed them. Realizing they weren't going to win the argument, they reluctantly headed to Fort William with the soldiers.

On their way through the gates, they passed a familiar face coming out of the fort.

"Dari?!" Annie exclaimed.

The sepoy looked up, startled to hear his name being called.

"Please help us," she begged.

Realizing who she was, Dari shrugged his shoulders and walked away as General Carnac and Thomas Webb came out to meet them.

"Ah, Mrs. Door, I see you have met my sepoy." Dari got on his horse and rode away. "Wasn't he one of the very people you came to save?"

"What did you do?" Annie said, trying to figure out what was going on.

Carnac clapped his hands together in jubilation. "Never mind that, I am just so delighted! Qasim has literally handed the entire region over to us."

"What do you want from us?"

"I do not think we got off on the right foot. I am John Carnac, Brigadier General and Commander of the Honourable East India Company." He saluted her in a mocking way. "And this is Lieutenant Colonel Thomas Webb. I have been told you are Annie." Carnac took a long look at Colt. "The sepoy said nothing about you having a son. And what is your name, young man?" He offered his hand, but Colt didn't take it.

"Colton James Door," Colt nervously replied.

Annie stepped in front of Colt. "Just tell me what you want."

"That is what I love about American women, always straight to the point," Carnac chuckled. "So different than what we are used to in England. It's refreshing, isn't it, Thomas?"

Webb chuckled exuberantly.

Carnac continued. "Where were you headed? And do not lie to me. We certainly would not want anything to happen to this fine boy." Carnac walked over to Colt and placed his hand firmly on Colt's shoulder.

"Trichy." Annie replied quickly.

"Why?"

"We are going to go see a friend at St. John's."

"St. John's? What did I just hear about St. John's?" Carnac thought about where he had heard that name before. "Yes, now I've got it. The new school just opened up." Carnac gleefully remarked as he released his grip on Colt. An idea began to brew in his mind.

"Great. Can we be going now?" Annie took Colt by the arm and started to walk away. They were stopped immediately.

"Your son, yes, I do not have any need for him. But you, my dear Annie, could be of great assistance. You see, I'm having trouble communicating with our sepoys. I don't speak Bengali very well, but I know you do. You could be our first official English teacher at Fort William."

"I am not going to help you do anything."

"That's not the response I was looking for . . . Thomas, may I have your sword."

"Of course, sir," Webb handed Carnac his sword.

"Please bring the boy forward." The soldiers pushed Colt closer to Carnac who rested the blade on Colt's shoulder near his throat.

"Stop! I will do whatever you want. Just don't touch my son."

"She is learning." Carnac shoved Colt to the ground before returning Webb's sword.

"You get him to Trichy, and I will teach whatever language you want."

Carnac mulled it over. "Deal," he finally said. "You are a shrewd negotiator. We have a shipment of goods that needs to go near there anyway. Hubert and Lawrence, take this young man to the captain, and inform him he is to be taken directly to St. John's in Tiruchirappalli."

Two of the soldiers seized Colt and they attempted to lead him away.

"Let me at least walk him to the ship," Annie cried out.

"Very well." Carnac replied.

"I'm going to walk with them. I want make sure Mrs. Door doesn't try to pull a fast one," Webb jeered.

"Make it quick. We've got a lot of work to do." Carnac said before he marched back to his office.

The soldiers let go of Colt, and Annie rushed over to him, wondering if this would be the last time she would ever see her son. She held on, making the moment last.

"He said, 'make it quick,'" Webb barked.

With no other choice than to comply, Annie and Colt proceeded to the docks. Webb, Hubert, Lawrence, and the other soldiers monitored their every move, eliminating any chance of escape. The welcoming breeze was gone, and the sun beat down on their heads refusing to offer any solace. Before, the harbor felt like a place of freedom; now it had become anything but.

"I want to stay here with you," Colt pleaded.

Annie stopped moving and held his face with her hands.

"Right now, being with Peter is the safest place for you. As soon as . . ." *Crack!* Out of nowhere, the butt of a rifle walloped the back of Annie's head. Unconscious, she fell helplessly to the ground.

"Time's up," Webb declared, holding a gun in his right hand.

"Mom!" Colt made a lunge at Webb, only to be caught by two soldiers.

"Aggression, that's good. You are going to need it where you are going. Southern India is not for the faint of heart."

"I'm not going anywhere!" Colt kicked his leg, landing one right to the shin of Hubert, who howled in pain.

"That is enough!" Webb bellowed. Annie finally stirred, and Webb pointed his rifle at Colt.

"What are we going to do with him, sir?" Hubert said after Colt was finally restrained.

"Kill me," Colt declared.

"No, I couldn't do that. Plus, it would bring much sorrow to your mother, and we have a great use for her.

If we keep you alive, she will work for us and do what we need her to do. Per her request, you will be sent to Trichy, and you will never return here, nor will you attempt to contact her. You will receive a proper education and possibly, one day, make something of yourself," Webb said cheerfully. Then he lowered his voice, "And don't try to pull any funny business like your father did. We took care of him, and we can just as easily take care of you." Webb pushed Colt away. "Get this bastard on the next ship to Madras."

After he heard Webb's threat, Colt didn't try to resist as Hubert and the other soldiers drug him away. Annie, clearly dazed, hadn't realized what was happening. She was lifted to her feet by Webb. All activities on the docks had ceased as everyone stared in astonishment at what had just taken place.

"What are you looking at? Everyone back to work!" Webb shouted.

Mouths were agape as Annie was whisked away to Fort William and out of sight, the gates closing behind her. Lieutenant Hubert marched Colt down the biggest dock. They passed a ship that had already been unloaded and made their way onto a packed one. It was scheduled to set sail at sundown. Dragging Colt aboard, Hubert urgently gave orders to the captain about taking him south. The captain vehemently protested about space and a lack of rations aboard the ship. He was swiftly shut down with the familiar phrase of "General's Orders." He reluctantly agreed to take Colt.

The boat wasn't quite as big as a typical cargo ship.

It had more cabins under the deck and the EIC used it for transportation between the three major ports, Calcutta, Madras, and Bombay. The first mate walked Colt through the interior of the ship, passing by sepoys, sailors, and prisoners. Finally, they stopped at the last door on the starboard side. It was a windowless room with a cot and a lamp sitting on a nightstand. There was also a bucket that would serve as his latrine. As soon as he stepped inside, the door was locked behind him. Colt pounded on the door, demanding to be released, begging to see his mother. His cries went unanswered. Exhausted, he fell onto the bed in a crumbled heap. He hoped he would wake up, and this nightmare would be over. Little did he know, his journey had only just begun.

TWELVE

Hours passed by before the boat finally left the docks. Colt stared at the ceiling, trying to collect his thoughts. All he could hear was, "We took care of him, and we can just as easily take care of you." He shivered as the words echoed in his mind. Raucous rapping interrupted his reflection. The door opened and a Bengali man stepped inside with a plate of potatoes and a glass of water. He set them on the floor without making eye contact. He then shut the door and locked it. Colt didn't realize how hungry he was until he took the first bite. It wasn't much, but at least he had food. Things could definitely be worse.

Colt remembered seeing Madras on a map, but he had no idea how long it would take to actually get there. The days unfolded like clockwork. Once a day there would be a knock at the door and the same sepoy delivered food.

It usually consisted of potatoes or rice and sometimes cabbage. Every third day, his old bucket would be replaced with a new one.

Weeks went by before the ship slowed down. Then one day it stopped completely. Relief came over Colt. He heard the lock click. He expected to see the same man but instead it was the first mate who initially had brought him to the cell. All he said was, "The Cap'n wants to see you," and walked out. Colt followed behind him and when he came up from below deck, he was astounded at what he saw: the port of Madras was now before him. It was entirely different than Fort William and much larger. Fort William was a stronghold of the East India Company, but this was a global port where French, Dutch, and Portuguese trade ships could be seen. However, even with all of the other ships, the harbor was still under control of the EIC.

As Colt studied the new landscape, the captain approached him along with two EIC soldiers who weren't over the age of twenty.

"Son, I don't know what you did to be here. Nor do I care. All I know is that I have to get you to Trichy."

"You don't have to take me anywhere. I'll find my own way," Colt calmly responded.

"That's not how it works around here. I got orders to take you to Trichy and that's where you're gonna go."

Colt considered arguing with him, but after being in the fresh air for the first time in so long, he decided against it.

"This is Private Bronson and Private Leslie. They

have just joined the Company. They will be escorting you to your new home." The two young soldiers didn't look happy about their first assignment as the captain continued speaking. "You won't be giving them any trouble, now, will you?"

"No, sir."

"Very good," the captain tipped his hat and away he went, leaving Colt with Bronson and Leslie.

THIRTEEN

February 1764
St. John's School, Tiruchirappalli
1,250 miles south of Fort William

"Look at verse one," came the instruction. "'But it displeased Jonah exceedingly, and he was very angry.' Those are heavy words. I wonder what he was so angry about, especially after such an unbelievable miracle had just taken place."

There was a knock at the door and a room full of boys looked up to see an elderly nun stick her head into the classroom.

"Father, I am sorry to interrupt you, but a situation has come up."

Peter walked out to see her, and she whispered

something to him. He came back and addressed the class with a disconcerting look on his face.

"I'm sorry, but that will be all today, gentlemen. Finish chapter four and be ready in case there is a quiz tomorrow."

The students groaned.

"I said, 'in case.'" He turned to the nun. "Sister Martha, please take the boys outside and then meet me back at my office."

Peter walked down the hallway where he found two soldiers waiting for him. Behind them was a young man whose eyes were fixed on a lonely crucifix hanging on the wall.

"Please come in." Peter opened the door to his office and they all went inside. Bronson and Leslie sat down while Colt stood by the window staring at the boys who were now playing on the lawn.

How can I help you, gentlemen?" Peter inquired.

"We've come from Madras. We were ordered here by General Carnac of the East India Company to bring this young man to you. His name is Colton Door. His mother is employed by the Company," Bronson recited while Peter attempted to grasp all of the information. Sister Martha returned and stood silently in the doorway.

"And why isn't his mother or father dropping him off here?"

"We are just following orders, sir. Will you take him?"

"Of course!" he stated emphatically.

The British soldiers gave Peter a half-hearted salute and left.

"Martha, will you take the rest of my appointments today?"

"Yes, Father, no problem at all," Sister Martha agreed as she left Colt and Peter alone.

"Can I get you some tea?"

Colt nodded, but his attention was on a game of cricket that had just begun. Peter rummaged around until he found a tea kettle and put it onto a stove.

Peter set a tin of biscuits on the table. "Here, eat these. I'm sure you are hungry."

"Thank you, sir," Colt softly responded, leaving the window.

"Please, call me Peter."

Colt sat down and slowly nibbled on the biscuits. The kettle whistled, and Peter poured two cups.

"Sugar?"

"Yes, please."

Peter put a spoonful of sugar into Colt's cup and placed it before him. Colt drank it ever so slowly and continued to eat the biscuits. He stopped and stared up at the bookshelf, recognizing some of the titles. Peter sipped on his tea, wondering how his friend's son had ended up in his office.

"My mom shared with me the letter you wrote," Colt finally said.

A wave of guilt swept over Peter.

"They took her away. Just like that. . ." Colt stared off into space.

"Who did?"

"The EIC."

"I don't understand."

"I don't either," Colt said, almost inaudibly.

Peter's mind was going a thousand miles a minute. He had no idea what could have happened. He wanted to ask a dozen questions, but he waited for Colt to continue. After draining the last drop of tea, Colt shared with him everything that had happened in the last few months. The more of the story Peter heard, the more responsible he felt for Colt's loss. If he hadn't written the letter, John might still be alive.

—⁓○

Peter showed Colt around the property, which was about three and a half acres. There was an open area for recreation next to a grove of trees which offered a nice bit of shade. The church was named after St. John the Apostle, which—unfortunately for Colt—would be a constant reminder of his father. The building itself included two classrooms, an office, and a dormitory where students stayed. There was also a chapel which was mainly used on Sundays and open to the community of Tiruchirappalli.

Not far from the main building was a parsonage where Peter lived and would also serve as Colt's new home. The humble house had two bedrooms and a kitchen.

"It is not much, but it's comfortable. You will take the room on the left. I've been using it for storage. Let me get that stuff out of there."

Colt walked around the place. It wasn't the cabin, but it was cozy, and it was better than being locked up in the bottom of a ship. As Peter carried out a crate of dusty textbooks, Colt got onto the bed without taking his clothes off.

"Okay, that should be about it," Peter said as he stuck his head into the room. But Colt was already fast asleep.

FOURTEEN

Colt followed Peter into a classroom full of boys who were laughing and talking. Everyone became quiet when they saw the new face. All of the students were British, except for one who had much darker skin than the others. There were twelve students in all, ranging in ages from eleven to fifteen.

"Good morning, boys. We have a new student today. His name is Colt and he has just moved to Trichy. Everyone, please, make him feel right at home."

Peter showed Colt to an open chair near the back of the room. As Colt made his way to his seat, a couple of the boys introduced themselves, including the boy with the darker skin.

"Hi, I am Henri. I have only been here for two weeks. It's nice to meet you. Where are you from?"

"America."

"America! Why did you come all the way here?"

"Okay, let's get back to our reading from yesterday. Where did we leave off?" Peter addressed the class, inadvertently saving Colt from answering the question.

A student named Rupert in the front of the class spoke up. "We were supposed to have finished chapter four."

"Ah, yes, thank you, Mr. Carlson. I am not even going to ask who actually read it. So, I'll just assume we all did. Let's back up. Can someone tell me how chapter three ended?"

Peter scanned the room for hands. No one volunteered, so he called on Henri who was busy drawing in his notebook.

"Mr. Dupleix, what happened at the end of chapter three?"

"Chapter three? I, uh, uh . . . I don't remember. I was too busy focusing on chapter four," Henri said, which elicited a roar of laughter from the class.

"I'm sure you were," Peter smirked. "Can someone help him out?"

"The people of Nineveh were ultimately saved from destruction," Charles, another student, answered.

"Outstanding, Mr. Wellington . . . and just for the sake of recap, who were the Ninevites?"

"They were one of Israel's enemies."

"And what was Nineveh the capital city of?"

There were again no hands except for Charles.

"Please tell me someone knows besides Mr. Wellington."

"The Assyrian Empire," came a voice from the back of the room.

"Excellent, Colt, I'm impressed. The Assyrian Empire. And they were known for their infamous cruelty. It has been said they would scrape off the skin of their victims, and then place them outside to burn under the scorching heat of the sun." Peter animated this by suddenly grabbing Henri, which made him jump out of his seat. This again caused everyone to laugh.

"However, they turned from their pernicious ways," Peter continued. "But as we find out in chapter four our man Jonah, who we've been discussing for the past week, was not happy with their unbelievable turn around. He has just finished leading this incredible revival and now he is indignant. If Jeremiah or Ezekiel would have had this kind of response to one of their messages, they would have been ecstatic! One hundred and twenty thousand lives were spared, and Jonah was a big reason why. So please tell me, why was Jonah so upset?"

The students were silent and listened in awe.

"For some reason," Peter suggested, "Jonah clearly felt they were undeserving of this miraculous deliverance. Do you agree?"

"Absolutely, these people were beyond wicked! Jonah had every right to be angry!" Charles exclaimed.

"What are you talking about Charles? Jonah should have drowned at sea. He didn't even deserve to be alive in the first place." Henri fired back. Other classmates started to shout their opinions, each one passionate about their viewpoint.

"Brilliant perspectives, all of you," Peter chimed in before a heated argument really broke out. "This debate is precisely what you are going to write about this weekend. Please answer these two questions for me: number one, was Jonah justified in being upset? And number two, how do you respond when someone receives something good, when they don't deserve it?" With that final statement, the morning session ended for the day and the students filed out of the classroom.

"Let's go," Henri said to Colt. Colt was unsure of what to do and looked to Peter, who nodded and smiled. Colt followed Henri outside into the schoolyard.

"Is class always like that?" Colt asked.

"Yeah, Father Peter is awesome." Henri surveyed the courtyard. "Hey, do you play cricket?"

"I love cricket!"

And with that, Henri put his arm around Colt. "Let's show em' how it's done."

Henri rounded up the other boys and a game began. Peter walked outside to get some fresh air. As he stood on the steps of the school, Sister Martha came up beside him.

"Shall I fetch the boys for their meal?" She queried.

Peter observed Colt who had just stepped up to bat. He mashed the ball, scoring a run. The other kids, thoroughly impressed, congratulated him.

"No, that's okay, Martha. We are going to let the boys play a little longer than usual today."

"How was your first day?" Peter asked, as he dished out mashed potatoes and spinach.

"It was much better than I expected it to be," Colt replied. "I really like Henri. He seems different than the other boys."

"That is because his family is not British. His father is a French fur trader in Karaikal. He lives here with his mother in order to attend St. John's. His dad felt it would be best for him if he was placed in an English-speaking school."

"How often does he see his dad?"

"Not very often, maybe once a year. It has been tough for him. You'll learn that everyone at St. John's has a story. But today certainly was the happiest I've seen Henri. I think you had something to do with that."

Hearing that made him feel good, "So, was this a pretty typical day? Morning session, break, afternoon session?"

"Yes, for the most part. Does it fit your schedule?" Peter joked.

"I think I can manage." Colt laughed for the first time in weeks.

After dinner, Colt retired to his room where his father's satchel was resting on the floor. A flickering candle threw strange shadows onto the wall. He missed his parents terribly. His thoughts floated back to the discussion in class today. All he knew about Jonah was that he supposedly was in the belly of a giant fish and survived. He didn't know Jonah had been sent to preach to his people's enemy. He hadn't heard the rest of the story until today. *How would he have responded?* He only had to think for a second because he already knew the answer. Jonah had every reason in the world to be furious. Taking some paper from a nearby drawer, he began to write as the anger inside of him burst forth onto the page.

FIFTEEN

The weeks and months passed by, and Colt became more accustomed to life at Trichy. There had been no word from his mother—not that he necessarily expected to hear anything from her. He thought about writing to her. But after Webb's threat, he wasn't about to take any chances. He had seen firsthand what the EIC was capable of, and he didn't want anything to happen to her. In fact, he tried to forget about what had happened, but that proved to be impossible. Nevertheless, he tried his best to live life as normally as he could.

Colt's best friend at school was Henri. They played cricket together almost every single day. He really did enjoy being at St. John's. It was nice to be in an actual school again. He hadn't experienced that since he was back in America. Everyone was very welcoming toward him. For the most part, all of the students were pretty much in the same boat as he was. Almost all of them had lost one or both parents—soldiers weren't the only casualties of war.

As time went on, Colt was able to hear his classmates' stories. It didn't take the pain of missing his parents away, but it showed him that he wasn't the only one who had suffered great loss. Peter taught them suffering was not only unavoidable, but it was an invaluable part of the human experience. Colt had become really close to Peter and looked up to him. Every evening around the dinner table, they would have engaging discussions which often lasted late into the night.

Colt could tell why his dad had been such close friends with Peter. He was very kind and had a great sense of humor. Peter joked that if it wasn't for him, his parents never would have met. Colt only knew that when his dad was at university in Scotland, he had met his mother on the banks of the River Thames. But that was only half of the story. Peter shared the rest. What happened was Peter met John while they both were attending King's College in Aberdeen. One fall break, Peter had taken John to his family's home in Gloucester. While they were in England, Peter wanted to give John a tour of London. On their last evening in the city, John met Annie.

It had been an unusually warm autumn afternoon, and John decided to take a walk. He ended up near the water, which is where Annie was. Annie, originally born in Massachusetts, was with her family for an extended holiday. Annie, like John, also wanted to take a walk by the water that day. As they were passing each other, they both exchanged pleasantries and were both initially shocked when neither one heard a British accent. They hit it off and ended up talking that night for hours. John was so smitten by her that he never went back to Gloucester, let alone Scotland. In fact, he ended up touring Europe with her family. He asked her to marry him in France near the Palace of Versailles. He convinced her to move back to his family farm in Pennsylvania and the rest was history.

Colt loved hearing the story and often had Peter retell it. He admired his dad's boldness and his mother's courage to leave her family. He marveled at the love they had for one another. He also was amazed when he found out Peter's story and the life he had given up in England to come to India.

Peter had moved to Trichy to work at St. John's much to the chagrin of his father, a wealthy cloth merchant. Peter's dad wanted him to take over the family business. Instead, Peter chose to leave everything because he wanted to help care for the orphans of British soldiers in India. He had heard heart-wrenching stories of what some of the kids had gone through due to the aftermath of all the fighting. He wanted to make a difference, and St. John's afforded him that opportunity.

"I felt a calling I could not explain," Peter shared—which was the same thing Colt had heard his father say time and time again.

As the years progressed, the school blossomed, but the same could not be said for the people of India. The EIC secured another major victory when Mir Qasim and his army were decimated in the town of Buxar. Even with the help of the armies of the Nawab of Awadh and Mughal Emperor Shah Allam II, they were still swiftly defeated. The outcome may have been different if the Mysoreans or the Marathas would have joined them instead of engaging in their own affairs. But the alliance never formed, and now a new treaty would soon be implemented.

SIXTEEN

August 1765
Fort William

John Carnac and Thomas Webb watched in anticipation as Robert Clive made his way through the halls of Fort William and into his old quarters. Sailing from London, Clive's ship had arrived earlier that morning. It had been a long time since Robert Clive had been in the office, but his fingerprints were still all over the place. Clive, normally known for his brooding, was the happiest he had been in a while.

"I hope you didn't get too comfortable in this chair, John," Clive said to General Carnac who sat down facing the old desk.

"Never, sir, I knew you would be back, and I

looked forward to your return," Carnac said through a forced smile.

"I knew you wouldn't be able to duplicate what I have accomplished here. But I must say I was pleasantly surprised when I heard about Munro's victory at Buxar. You have set us up perfectly, John! This treaty will change everything."

The Treaty of Allahabad would be signed the following week, giving the East India Company a complete stranglehold and unprecedented power over the entire northeast. Bengal, Bihar, Orissa, and everything in between now belonged to the EIC. The once small corporation had conquered the mighty Mughal Empire— at one point, the richest empire in the world. The EIC allowed Emperor Shah Allam II to hold onto his title and allowed Shuja-ud-Daulah to return to Awadh—as long as they both continued to pay the EIC annually. As for Mir Qasim, his fate wasn't as fortunate.

After the treaty had been signed and the days passed, the once exciting victory waned in Clive's mind as he considered future preparations and possibilities. He was back in the office with Carnac and Webb, who were discussing the company's next course of action.

"Isn't it time to reap our reward?" Webb surmised. "We have worked extremely hard over the years and it's time we were paid handsomely. Wouldn't you agree?"

"We mustn't forget the shareholders. At the end of the day, we report to them," Carnac replied dutifully as he sipped on a glass of brandy.

"What have they done? We are the ones risking our

arses living in this hellhole, constantly battling the heat, snakes, and mosquitoes."

"Dammit!" Clive pounded the desk and launched his pipe across the room, sending tobacco and ashes flying. "Would the both of you shut up! You are like spoiled school children arguing about who gets the first spoonful of Christmas pudding!"

Webb and Carnac clammed up as if they were being scolded by a parent. Clive stood up from the desk and approached Carnac, looking as if he might hit him, only to brush a piece of dandruff from his shoulder.

"Of course, the shareholders who have placed their utmost faith in us will be compensated," Clive said rolling his eyes. "And you . . ." Clive glared at Webb. "I heard about your stunt in the market with that Indian girl." He slapped him across the face before continuing. "How stupid can you be? We are trying to gain trust from the locals. Something like that could have caused a revolt!"

"It's been dealt with, sir," Carnac said, coming to Webb's defense.

"Good. But if I hear another outburst like that, *both* of you will be removed."

Neither Webb nor Carnac stirred, both understanding the gravity of the situation.

"Now on a much different tone, it's true, we have indeed become Nawabs. But now the real work begins."

"What do you mean, sir? The entire northeast is firmly within our grasp," Webb stated incredulously.

"The people of India have handed us the authority merely by believing that we are mightier than they. It's all in their heads. The minute they wake up from their slumber, it's over for us. It's our job to keep them asleep. But now the problem is, they are being roused by Hyder Ali. His army grows daily, and we've done very little about it. Do you understand?"

"Yes, sir. I'm sorry, sir," Webb apologized.

"Thomas, grab a quill and paper. I have a few ideas I would like you to write down." He said, pacing around the room.

"Of course, sir."

"As we've previously stated," Clive began, "this treaty was a huge step in my . . . I mean, the company's future. However, we cannot get caught up in the past. We have a window of time and we must act swiftly. Number one, I want to build our military. I want more sepoys fighting for us than the entire British army. Number two, I want to expand our opium production. The Chinese are killing us in the trade wars. We need something to counter with. Number three, I want to increase the number of slaves we have here. There are millions of people living in this country, and I don't see why we can't profit off those numbers. And lastly, number four, taxation; we will now be collecting taxes directly from the people of the region. Someone has got to pay for this operation, and it certainly isn't going to be us."

Webb scribbled away, making sure he wrote down Clive's plan moving forward.

"Sir, if I may?" Carnac spoke up.

"What could you possibly want to add, John?" Clive chided.

"If we tax the people and our profits skyrocket, it will bring a lot of attention to what we are doing here."

"You certainly are a foolish man. Why would that be a bad thing?"

"Stay with me, sir."

"What's your point?"

"Not everyone in England is happy with what we've accomplished here. And our critics are growing by the day. A bigger operation means more investors, which could lead to more inquiries. It isn't a problem if the money is rolling in, but what would happen if it ever were to stop?

"Why would it stop?" Clive asked.

"Suppose one day the people can't afford the tax. Or the crops fail, and we show a quarterly loss. What will the investors say then?" Carnac reasoned. Clive hesitated and Carnac stood up, continuing to speak. "What if this happens multiple quarters in a row? We could be in quite a quandary in a hurry. I have no problem with anything you've said, sir. I would just advise that we slow it down."

"Slow it down? Now? Right when we've just reached the pinnacle of our power!"

"I just think we should show a steady increase and build up our reserves."

"I do not have all the time in the world. I will be heading back to England sometime in the next two years."

"Sir," Carnac protested.

"That's enough nonsense from you. We will not slow anything down. It's full steam ahead from here on out. Do I make myself clear?"

"Yes, sir," Webb responded immediately.

"John?"

"Yes, sir," Carnac replied, begrudgingly.

"Okay. Now that we've covered that. It's high time we focus on Ali. He's one of the last obstacles standing in our way."

SEVENTEEN

May 1769
St. John's School, Tiruchirappalli
1,250 miles south of Fort William

"The cat was on the cot wearing a coat. 'A' is pronounced C-ahhh-T. 'O' is pronounced C-awee-T. 'OA' is pronounced C-ohhh-T. Say them with me."

"C-ahhh-t, C-awee-t, C-ohhh-T," the classroom full of six- and seven-year-olds stumbled through the words.

"Very good, everyone! Today, we are going to learn about vowels," Colt said as he smiled at the kids in front of him.

He had a hard time grasping that he was in his third year of teaching and that he had been at St. John's for almost six years already. Due to British expansion in India, the school had grown by leaps and bounds. Although they continued to care for orphans, enrollment was open, and more and more students came through their doors. As this happened, Colt had taken on more responsibility. He was happy to do it. He enjoyed teaching and Peter needed the help.

Sister Martha came to fetch the kids for their meals. Normally, Colt would take a break as well, but today he had work to do. He sat at his desk as he prepared for the afternoon session with the older students. He had trouble concentrating and soon found himself staring out the window, something he did often. His mind wandered back to the village in Burdwan. He thought about Zara and what she might look like now. He didn't know if she was still there or not. After the treaty of Allahabad, everything had changed. Peter had shared with Colt all that had happened in Buxar, and what it meant for all of India. The people's only hope now was for Hyder Ali and the Mysorean army to stand its ground in the south.

Colt heard footsteps approaching and snapped out of the daze. He went back to the arithmetic he planned on teaching in an hour.

"Good afternoon, Colt," Peter said as he walked into the room. "I've just received another letter from a parent raving about how much their son enjoys having you as his teacher."

"They are good kids," Colt said as he brushed off the compliment.

"They *are* good kids, but what you've done is

remarkable. With the way we are growing, we will have to hire more teachers."

As Colt continued talking to Peter, he heard his name being shouted. They were both shocked to see Henri entering the classroom.

"Colt! A new treaty has been signed in Madras! War has ceased!" Henri exclaimed, not realizing Peter was also in the room. "Oh, hi, I'm sorry to interrupt, sir. I did not see you there."

"You do not have to call me 'sir' anymore. You have been out of here for three years."

"Yes, sir. I mean, Peter." Henri focused his attention on Colt. "Colt, listen to me. The Mysores held their ground and the EIC has been subdued in the southeast. Now is our time to move."

"I'm not sure, Henri. That was a long time ago."

"Colt for years, all you've talked about is how you wanted to sail a boat to Fort William. We finally have a golden opportunity, and you are telling me you don't want to go now! What changed?"

"I can't just leave Peter like that. He needs my help," Colt insisted.

"Colt, I'll be okay."

"What about the school?"

"The school will be fine. Henri is right. We've been waiting for something like this to happen. This is your chance."

"We'll go to Karaikal to see my dad. He'll know where we can get a boat to sail north," Henri said proudly.

Colt glanced out the window again. "I knew this day

would come. I just did not expect it to happen like this."

Peter placed his hand on Colt's shoulder, reassuring him. "Sometimes the unexpected way ends up being the best way."

⌁

Colt leafed through old papers in his room deciding what would go with him on the upcoming trip. He came across a stack that included his first essay that he had ever written at St. John's. It had been on Jonah. He read the beginning as anger started to swell inside of him. He put it down before the emotion overtook him. After looking over the rest of the papers he determined it was probably best to leave them here. He chose to take some blank pages along with a quill and inkwell instead.

As Colt finished up packing, he picked up his father's Bible and debated whether or not to include it in his already stuffed satchel. He hadn't opened it once since he brought it to St. John's, nor did he have a desire to. As much as he admired Peter, and his parents for that matter, he just couldn't get on board with what they believed. The idea of some higher being sounded like a great idea, but there was far too much evil in the world for him to accept something like that. His dad risked everything for his faith, and it got him killed. But it was one of the few items he had that previously belonged to his father. Reluctantly, he put it back in the bag.

"How is it coming?" Peter asked as he came through the door.

"Can I ask you a question?" Colt asked.

"Of course."

"Do you remember my first day of class when we talked about Jonah?"

"Yeah, I actually do. What about him?"

"I know Jonah was really angry after all of those people were rescued supernaturally. But, how did the story end?"

"The text doesn't say, so we don't truly know. Some scholars are convinced that Jonah is the author of the book, and he chose to leave the ending like that on purpose."

"Why would he do that?"

"By leaving it open-ended, he's allowing us to put ourselves in his shoes."

Colt contemplated what Peter had said. "Do you think he came around?" Colt asked.

"I would like to think so, especially if he was indeed the author. What made you bring him up in the first place?"

"I was going through my old stuff and came across an essay I had written about him."

"I remember that essay. You argued that Jonah had every right to be angry. Very compelling writing."

"I would say the same thing again today," Colt said. He felt the heat rise behind his collar.

"Colt, I should have said this to you a while ago. I just figured time would have healed your heart. I'm so sorry about everything that's happened to you. You did nothing wrong. But you have to understand, holding onto your anger won't bring your parents back."

Colt glared at Peter, stunned he would say such a thing.

"You don't know what I've been through."

"You're right. I don't. But I do know that if you don't let it go, your anger will destroy you."

Colt was fuming now. "This whole time I thought you were on my side and now I can see how blind I was!"

"Colt!"

"You're even running this stupid school for them."

"What are you saying?"

"You are just a pawn of the EIC."

"You know that's not true. Come on, it's your last night. I have something I want to give you."

"It is true. And you know what else is true?"

"What else, Colt?" Peter asked as tears formed in his eyes.

"If you never would have written that letter to my parents asking them to come to this detestable place, they would still be alive."

Peter reached for Colt.

"No. Get out of my way. I should have left a long time ago." Colt grabbed his bag and stormed past him, heading straight for the door.

EIGHTEEN

Henri was taken aback when he found Colt knocking at his front door, seeing as they weren't supposed to leave until the following morning. Colt was in no mood to explain why he had come early. They ate a quick snack of rice and beans and talked about their upcoming travel plans. As ready as Colt was to leave Trichy, he couldn't escape the gnawing feeling he felt inside. He regretted what he had said, but Peter triggered everything that had been shut up within him. The more he ruminated, the worse he felt.

Over the last six years, no one had sacrificed more for him than Peter had. He treated him like a son and allowed him to move into his home. He taught him, fed him, and gave him a job. He knew he still had time to go back and make it right. The tug of war continued in his mind all night long. But when morning came he pushed the feelings down and focused solely on making it to Fort William, his heart icing over with every step.

Karaikal was due east of Trichy. It sat on the Bay of Bengal. If they were able to hike around ten miles a day, they would be there in just over a week. Aside from seeing a pair of king cobras and hearing the eerie cries of the dholes, the beauty of the wildlife helped soothe Colt's conscience. He loved watching chital. The spotted deer travelled in herds and were seen almost daily. Another impressive animal that they encountered was the gaur. Blown away by the size of the Indian bison, they made sure to stay out of their way.

When water was found, the travelers tossed in a line, hoping to catch a sole or emperor fish—but they mostly ended up with sardines. They didn't complain; they were just glad they had caught something. As they sat around the fire at twilight, a large creature was spotted in the distance.

"Is that a . . .?" Henri whispered.

"*Shhh* . . ." Colt put his finger to his mouth.

"Can they swim?"

"Oh yeah."

The tiger looked up but paid them no attention. He licked the water as they held their breath. He bounded off into the forest as quickly as he appeared, his majestic coat shone in the moonlight.

"I have never been that close to one before," Henri said before he realized Colt wasn't seated next to him anymore. Henri stood up to look for him when Colt suddenly grabbed him, scaring him half to death. He dropped his fish and bolted in fear.

"That's not funny," Henri said as he walked back cautiously, picking up the remains of his dinner off of the ground.

"Yes it was. You should have seen your face."

"Okay, maybe it was a little bit funny," Henri said as they both started laughing.

The stars lit up the night sky as the sound of crickets filled the air.

"Man! That fish was good!" Colt exclaimed.

"If only I had a little paprika to put on it!"

"You would ask for paprika," Colt said, teasing him, "Hey, I am just thankful we are eating something. It was looking bleak there for a second."

"After you caught that massive one, we went on a roll."

Henri sprawled out on the ground—exhausted—as Colt stoked the fire, sending embers into the air like fireflies.

"Do you think you will ever go back to America?"

"Hopefully, one day."

"What do you miss the most?"

"Walking in the fields with my grandpa."

As Colt reminisced about his old life in Pennsylvania, faint snoring was heard in the background.

"Henri, are you awake?"

There was no answer. Colt understood what that meant. Chuckling to himself, he rolled over and gazed up at the stars. He felt complete tranquility and was soon dreaming about being back on the farm.

Nineteen

Karaikal
1,230 miles south of Fort William

Karaikal was finally spotted on the horizon. A town that had exchanged hands between the French and British over the years now belonged again to the French. It was certainly a welcoming sight for Henri who hadn't been back in years. For Colt, it was like being in an entirely new country. He had never been around so many French soldiers at once. Once they arrived inside of the city, they went straight to Henri's father's shop.

Darte's Trading Post. The freshly painted wooden sign hung above a window. Henri opened the door and a bell jingled above alerting Darte that someone had just entered his store. The large and gregarious man was astonished to see his son standing in the entryway. The two embraced warmly. Henri introduced Colt to his father, telling him that he wanted to buy a boat; this delighted Darte who had spent much time on the high seas as a younger man.

"Thanks for bringing him home. Come, come, you must be hungry," Darte said in a thick French accent while leading them to a back room. He brought out a loaf of bread and poured them each a glass of red wine. "This just arrived from Bordeaux."

Dante swirled the glass in his hand, taking a big sniff before sipping. Henri and Colt did likewise, pretending to know what they were doing. Colt listened as the two conversed in French. Henri hung on to every word his father said. Colt didn't mind, he was just thankful he would be sleeping indoors.

"So, my son says you are in the market for a boat," Darte finally addressed Colt.

Colt nodded.

"I'd recommend you go to Pondicherry. You'll find a better selection there. Their harbor is much bigger. Look for a man named Deshi. I've known him for years. His spot is in the heart of the docks. You can't miss him. Tell him Darte sent you. He will take care of you."

"That sounds great! We will definitely look for him."

"We?" Darte questioned.

"Hey, Dad, Colt and I are going to head upstairs to get some rest," Henri interjected. Colt, unsure of Darte's response, followed Henri upstairs into a modest apartment to catch up on some much-needed sleep.

The next morning, Darte sent Colt and Henri to

the harbor to drop off a load of pelts to be sent back to France. While they were on their way, they were stopped by a mysterious woman in a red and black checkered dress wearing a black bandana around her forehead and large, ivory hoop earrings. Her hair was raven, and she had piercing green eyes. The woman was fascinating, and Colt couldn't stop looking at her. There was something very evil about her and yet equally alluring at the same time. His soul told him to keep walking, but her mystique drew him in.

"I've been looking for you," she said. Her finger brushed the side of Colt's cheek, causing him to shake with adrenaline. "But first I must tell him something."

"*Dayan!*" Henri uttered under his breath, eliciting a wink from the enchantress. Taking Henri by the hand; she brought him close to her and whispered in his ear. His face turned white as a ghost. Colt couldn't hear a word that was said. When she finished, she put her finger to her lips. Henri automatically reached into his pocket and gave her a gold coin.

She then focused her full attention onto Colt. Exhilaration mingled with fear surged through him.

"I know you're dying to know what I told him. And you will find out soon enough. But first, let me have a look at you." The woman encircled Colt and started whispering to herself. The peculiar part was that her responses sounded as though she were actually talking to someone, but no one was there—that he could see.

Colt was instantly spooked. "Come on man, let's go."

"No," Henri pushed back. "You have to hear what she

has to say. She's incredible."

Henri was mesmerized.

The woman grabbed Colt's hand, and he jerked away from her, repulsed.

"What's the matter? You don't believe in this type of stuff anyway."

"You're right. I don't."

"You should, because it's real. Very real . . . your father believed." She paused and studied Colt's face, as if she were trying to read his mind.

Colt seized Henri's arm violently and turned to go. "I don't have time for this."

"It's too bad he was on the wrong side," she said matter-of-factly.

"You know nothing about my father," Colt roared back.

"I know he abandoned you. I also know bad things happen wherever you go."

"Shut up!"

"Don't you understand? The angrier you become, the clearer I can see."

She squinted as though she could see something far away.

"I am intrigued." She smiled and continued, "who is the fair-skinned man you were screaming at? I know it's not your father. All I know is that you are definitely blaming him for your father's death."

"It wasn't his fault."

"But you are telling him that it is," she said.

She could see that she had gotten to him. "It doesn't matter," she continued. "You don't have to tell me who he is." Her voice softened. "Look, Colt, I just want to help you."

"How do you know my name?"

The woman approached him. "I know a lot about you. I'm nothing like your father. As I said, I'm here to help you." She gently put her index finger in the middle of his forehead. "I just want to help you see."

Shockwaves reverberated throughout Colt's entire body, emanating from somewhere deep within his spine. She continued speaking, "If you let me, I can take all that pain away. I will make you so powerful, Colt, that no one will ever be able to hurt you again."

"It can't be that simple."

"Oh, but it is," she insisted. "That's the difference between me and your father. He makes everything so difficult. I make things easy. He takes away. I give. Can't you see it? Look how much he's taken from you already. Come with me, and I will share everything I have with you. I will teach you the secret knowledge that has existed from the beginning. Just say the words, and I'll fix everything." She put her finger in front of him again as she waited for his permission.

Colt closed his eyes and pondered everything she had proposed. It all sounded so good. As soon as he was about to accept her offer, his mother's face flashed before him in his mind, causing him to take a step back.

"What are you doing?" Her voice sounded slightly agitated.

"I . . . uhh . . ." Colt took another step back. His mother's smile came clearer into focus.

"Trust me," the woman hissed through clenched teeth.

"I can't!" he finally said as he turned away from her.

"You fool!" she snarled. "If you go through with this, there will be so much more pain that awaits you."

TWENTY

The following day, nothing was mentioned about the incident. When Colt finally brought it up, Henri refused to talk about it. Three more days went by, and Colt became more and more antsy. He was still shaken from the whole ordeal, and he wanted out of Karaikal. He needed answers, and knew he wouldn't have them if he didn't continue on his journey. But progress wasn't being made and each day felt like the same. Every morning, Colt and Henri would help out with tasks around the shop. At night, they would go to the local tavern and listen to a drunken Darte tell stories about his seafaring past and myriad rendezvous' in Paris. It was amusing in the beginning, but it got old quickly for Colt. Henri, on the other hand, was having the time of his life. He was perfectly content as time idly passed by.

After a week of the monotony, Henri finally broached

the subject.

"What if this was a bad idea?" Henri asked.

"What are you saying?"

"Maybe we should just stay here. We could live with my dad. He would have work for us."

"This entire trip was your idea!" Colt protested.

"Look, it was a bad idea."

"Wait. You didn't even tell him. I knew there was something up that first night."

"I know. I know. I'm sorry," Henri apologized.

"What about my mother?"

"You don't even know for sure she's still up there."

"I know she's up there," Colt insisted.

"I didn't think I was going to have to tell you this. But now I'm afraid there's no other choice." He looked down at the wooden floor. "Your mother is dead, Colt. That's what the woman told me." He mumbled.

Colt grabbed him. "What exactly did she say?"

"She said, 'His mother is dead' . . . and that I should stay here with my dad."

"You are going to believe that witch?"

"Yes, Colt. I am. She knew your name. She knew about your father. She even knew about Peter."

"Come on, Henri."

"Tell me then. How did she know about all that other stuff?"

"I don't know," Colt said angrily. "But she's lying about my mom. I know it."

"I don't think so."

"Come on, Henri. I need you!" Colt implored.

"I'm sorry, Colt. I can't."

Colt knew Henri had made up his mind and there was nothing he could do about it. He gathered his belongings.

"Just wait until tomorrow." Henri said.

"Too much time has already been wasted."

"Well, wait a second." Henri went into the other room and came back with an old machete. He handed it to Colt. "It belonged to a Maratha Warrior on my mom's side. It's not doing any good collecting dust. Take it, please."

Colt put the machete on his belt and walked out the door.

⤙

Using the Bay of Bengal as a guide, he began his trek up the Coromandel Coast toward Pondicherry. He was still enraged at Henri for backing out. Henri had been the one who had talked him into going on this trip in the first place. They were supposed to do this together, and now he was alone—again. He didn't believe the woman was telling the truth. But he didn't know for sure. He briefly considered going back to Trichy and foregoing the mission altogether. But he had come so far already and would continue. He made camp along the water.

The next morning, he was awakened by a pair of kites squawking over a dead fish that had washed up on the shore. He folded up his bed roll and headed out, but not before he took a dip in the sea. The warm water felt like a bath and he didn't stay in long.

He spent the majority of the day walking, and his legs were getting tired. Before he could find a spot to rest, he heard someone calling out to him.

"Hi, I'm Bandi. What's your name?"

Colt turned around and was surprised to see a teenager jogging to catch up with him. The young man set down a bag of books he had been carrying and, with a bright smile, stuck out his hand. Colt was unsure of what he wanted.

"What's your name? Where are you from?" the young man said in English.

"Colt." Colt looked around to see if this were some kind of trap. "I'm from America."

"Where are you headed?"

"North," Colt responded, convinced he was safe—but still, he didn't want to divulge any real information.

"What for?"

"Adventure."

For the time being, Bandi was satisfied with the answer. Colt changed the subject.

"You have very good English."

"Thanks," said Bandi. "When the British began to make their presence known in Pondicherry, my parents wanted me to learn it in case I would ever need it."

"I see," Colt said. "Well, it was nice to meet you." Colt walked forward, as if to signify the end to the conversation.

"Where are you staying tonight?"

"I was just going to sleep somewhere on the beach

again."

"No way! You are staying at my house. My father is going to want to meet you. He loves meeting new people."

"I was planning on setting up camp near here and calling it a day."

"Nonsense! You said you were looking for adventure," Bandi persisted. "Our place is not far. You can continue on your journey in the morning. It's just for one night."

Bandi would not take no for an answer, so Colt finally agreed to go.

⁓

Bandi was beside himself that Colt was coming to his house. He had never met an American, but had read stories about the "New World" and the otherworldly tales that had supposedly unfolded there. In his mind, America was a mythical land and Colt was some kind of exotic creature. Colt was not used to receiving such treatment and, truth be told, it was uncomfortable. Nevertheless, he allowed Bandi to revel in his imagination. They had walked a little over half a mile when Bandi alerted Colt they had arrived.

TWENTY-ONE

Cuddalore
1,160 miles south of Fort William

Banana trees lined the lane leading up to a sprawling estate as a peacock marched past them flaunting his feathers. During their walk, Bandi shared that his father owned the majority of the sugarcane fields in the area, but Colt never dreamed they would live in such a palatial mansion. It had huge marble pillars in the front and an open porch that wrapped around the entire house. Bandi led him up the stairs toward massive rosewood doors inlaid with two golden tigers. This was by far the most impressive home he had ever been to.

As they entered into the palace, they were straight away met by one of Bandi's sisters, Sanjeeda. Her pet monkey sat on her shoulder and covered up his ears as she obnoxiously yelled about Bandi's late arrival. Immediately, a servant appeared and took the bag Bandi had been holding before disappearing down a long corridor. They entered into the living room and there was a huge winding staircase to the left.

"Momma's not going to be happy with you," Sanjeeda continued her rant. "You were supposed to be back a while ago." Bandi's mother came out with her other two daughters to see what all the fuss was about. The youngest was in her arms. Bandi's mother was very pretty and appeared to be around the age of forty.

"Bandi Gajendra Sharat!" she shouted. "What do you think you are doing coming home at this hour?"

She stopped speaking as soon as she realized that Colt was standing there. Her smile made him feel welcome. The middle daughter stood beside her, taking it all in. The toddler squirmed out of her mother's arms and scooted herself down the steps. Bandi ran and kissed his mother on the cheek.

"Please forgive my tardiness mother, this is Colt . . . Colt the *Mavirar*. He is going to stay with us before he heads off on his big adventure."

"It's a pleasure to meet you, Colt the Mavirar. I am so happy you are here. My name is Rimi."

"And I am Sanjeeda. This is my monkey, Sashi. Oh, and that's Nita and Kiki." She pointed to her sisters. Nita hid behind Rimi, while Kiki continued crawling slowly down the steps. She stopped at the last step and beamed up at him. Colt's heart began to melt.

"Prepare a room for him," Rimi ordered to a nearby servant. The servant nodded and dashed off. "Sanjeeda, please inform your father that your brother has a guest, an American man."

"Yes, Momma," Sanjeeda said before darting out of the room.

"Bandi, take Colt to his room and wash up. Dinner is in half an hour." Rimi excused herself and exited the room, taking the girls with her.

"Let's go, Colt the Mavirar."

"What does that mean anyway?

"It means, 'The Warrior.'"

—

Fresh water had been poured into a gold bowl by a full-length mirror, and a white towel was laid out next to it. There was a long, navy blue, linen tunic lying on the bed for him along with a pair of sandals. Large elephant tusks gilded with gold served as the primary decorations on the wall. Colt was awestruck by the lavishness of the room. He had never experienced so much wealth and opulence before. As he approached the mirror, he saw someone he didn't recognize. His once clean-shaven face had been replaced with a beard.

He put his hands into the stone basin and washed the dust and sweat off of his face. Out of respect for his hosts, he put on the clothes laid out for him, along with the sandals. Before he headed out, he explored the room and found another door leading to a balcony. He walked outside to catch a glimpse of the setting sun. Its fleeting rays covered a mango orchard on the backside of the property. It truly was one of the most beautiful sights he had ever seen. He sat down on a nearby bench to soak it all in. He couldn't help but to feel this moment had somehow been prepared for him. It was simply too perfect.

Colt left the room refreshed, but he couldn't stop tugging at his clothes. The traditional outfit was extremely comfortable, and it fit him like a glove, but he hadn't worn anything like it before. Trying to not think about how insecure he felt, he went to look for Bandi. Instead, he discovered another staircase that led back downstairs; he elected to take it. As soon as he reached the bottom, he was greeted by a leopard mount, its teeth snarling at him.

In the same room, there were more mounts: rhino, antelope, wild boar, and sambar deer. There were also different types of animal skin rugs on floor. Colt explored the area which led to another room filled with paintings. As he walked through admiring the rest of the extravagant art, he couldn't help but to notice something strange. All of the paintings were from France, and they didn't seem to fit in with the rest of the exotic collection. A servant saw him wandering around and motioned for him to follow. He was then led down another hallway to a solitary oak door.

TWENTY-TWO

The attendant knocked twice and the door swung wide open. Colt was brought into a grand dining hall where Bandi and his entire family were waiting for him. Servers dressed in white lined the walls like statues. The stately room could have easily hosted over a hundred people.

"Colt!" Bandi exclaimed jumping up from the table. "You look great!"

The entire family rose from their seats, except for Bandi's father.

"Welcome, my good man. My son tells me that you are heading north, where specifically?"

"Calcutta," said Colt.

"You are a very brave man. Please forgive me; my English is not very good. My name is Sharat Desai." Then, to his middle daughter, "Nita, my love, would you please show our guest to his seat?"

Nita bashfully escorted Colt to the seat opposite of Sharat. Sharat snapped his fingers and immediately the servers sprang into action. A banana leaf was placed in front of Colt and all types of food were heaped onto it. *Chapati*—a type of flat bread; *Keerai Kootu*–a thick stew with spinach, lentils, and coconut; *Avial*—vegetables cooked with spices and coconut oil; *Sundal*—stir-fried chickpeas and curry leaves; *Chettinad Chicken*—a spicy, savory dish made with red chilies; and a lot of rice. The meal which sat before him looked like an edible rainbow. He couldn't wait to dig in!

Seeing there was no fork, Colt instinctively reached for the food with both of his hands. He felt a soft kick under the table from Bandi, gesturing to him that he needed to eat with his right hand only.

"This is delicious," Colt remarked, causing the girls to giggle.

"I am so glad you are enjoying it," Rimi said happily.

"And to think you were going to just sleep on the beach and eat more fish," Bandi joked.

"That would not have been a smart decision," Colt said, laughing.

"So, Colt, tell me. When did you come to our beautiful country?" Sharat asked.

"I came here a little over nine years ago."

"Nine years!" Sharat exclaimed. "That's quite a long time. I was under the impression you were here to hunt or explore."

As Colt began to explain, he was swiftly interrupted

with another question.

"What were you doing before you began your travels?"

"I used to be a schoolteacher."

"Where?"

"Trichy."

"What was the name of the school?"

"St. John's."

"That's an EIC school!"

Colt was instantly reminded of his last conversation with Peter and how he had said those exact words. However, hoping to avoid a technical argument, he went along with Sharat's assumption. "Yes, it is."

"Are you a sympathizer?" Sharat inquired austerely.

"No."

"But you taught their children?"

"Kids are kids."

"I see," Sharat wasn't convinced.

There was a moment of silence before Sanjeeda piped up. "Papa, tell Colt about the soldiers."

This topic was supposed to be a kept a secret and Sharat let his eldest daughter know by giving her a stern look.

"Yes, there is another detail about this place. It was used as a hideout for the French in their struggle with the EIC years ago. But I'm sure you already knew that." Sharat said sarcastically.

Bandi quickly changed the subject. "Sanjeeda, why don't you tell Colt about your pet monkey, Sashi." Receiving her opportunity for the spotlight, Sanjeeda eagerly told an exaggerated story of how she came to buy Sashi at the market and how she picked him out all by herself. The rest of the dinner went by amicably without any disturbances other than Sharat was very quiet, as if something was on his mind.

"Okay, girls, it's time for bed," Rimi finally announced.

"No, no, I want to stay up with Colt," Sanjeeda pleaded.

"You will see Colt tomorrow. Say goodnight."

"But, Mom!"

"Say 'goodnight.'"

"Goodnight, Colt."

"Goodnight, girls."

"It was a pleasure meeting you. We will see you in the morning." Rimi said.

With Kiki sound asleep in her arms, she left with Sanjeeda and Nita. Sharat promptly rose from the table and headed into the trophy room, followed by Bandi and Colt.

TWENTY-THREE

Billowing smoke rings rose from the edge of Sharat's lips. He smoked hookah—deep in thought on an oversized silk rug surrounded by comfortable pillows—while Colt and Bandi sat on a plush rug across from him. As was the custom, they waited for him to speak first.

"Something . . ." Sharat took a long hit, ". . . does not add up. You say you aren't with the EIC, yet you teach their children, and you are heading straight to their headquarters."

"I'm not in the EIC, sir."

"Then what are you heading up there for?"

Colt stared at the floor. "I'm looking for someone from my past."

Sharat slammed his fist on the ground in fury. "Stop lying to me, boy!"

"I'm not lying."

"You are spy!"

"I'm not a spy! I hate the EIC as much as you do."

Sharat took one last hit on the hookah. "Okay. I believe you," he said abruptly and stood up. "I'm going to retire for the evening. Goodnight." He walked over to Bandi and kissed him on the forehead. Before he was out of the door, he stopped and admired a mounted tiger, petting its head.

"Isn't he magnificent?" he said smiling. "This might be my favorite piece that I own. You see, most of the animals I have collected I had to go and find. But this one came right into my own backyard. He was found somewhere he shouldn't have been, and he paid a very dear price." He grinned diabolically at Colt and disappeared behind the door.

"Don't worry about him. I know you aren't in the EIC," Bandi said cheerfully.

"How do you know?" Colt asked reticently.

"That's easy," Bandi started giggling. "Everyone in the EIC has a British accent, you clearly don't!"

Colt laughed out loud as his anxiety dissipated, and the fast friends talked late into the night.

⌁

"I'm sorry my husband was not able to be here. He had to go into town early this morning. It was so nice to meet you. Here is some chapati and mangoes to take with you." Rimi said goodbye, handing him the food as Kiki waved.

"Bye, Colt! Sashi says 'bye' too!" Sanjeeda yelled. The pet covered its ears once again. Colt waved goodbye. Then, unexpectedly, Nita came running out of the house.

"Colt, wait!" He turned around, surprised to hear the very shy middle daughter calling his name. "I made this for you." She handed him a necklace with a small beaded tiger on it.

"Nita, how did you know this was my favorite animal?" He said amazed.

She shrugged her shoulders and blushed.

"I'm going to wear it right now." He put the necklace around his neck.

"I have something for you too," Colt continued. He got down on his knees, reached into his satchel, and pulled out the cricket ball Rafa had given him many years ago. "This used to belong to one of my best friends. I hope you have as much fun with it as we did." She gave him a big hug and then ran up the steps proudly to show her mother.

Colt took one final look at the home before he walked down the lane with Bandi. They stopped at the edge of the property. Bandi handed Colt a bag with an extra change of clothes, a rope, bananas, sugar, and lentil seeds. "A Mavirar never knows all he might need on his journey."

Colt was overwhelmed by the generosity of this young man; meeting Bandi had done something for his soul. For the first time in years, he was excited about the possibilities of the future. He too wanted to give him a token of his appreciation. Knowing his love for books, Colt handed Bandi his father's copy of *Pilgrim's Progress*. Bandi was overjoyed by the gift.

They embraced for the final time. Colt knew he had met Bandi for a reason and, with his hopes renewed, he headed to Pondicherry.

TWENTY-FOUR

Pondicherry
1,150 miles south of Fort William

Loud music and singing could be heard not too far away. Colt jogged ahead to see what was going on. Hundreds of people were dancing and making their way through the streets, but he couldn't tell why they were celebrating. He ducked through an alley in order to cut off the crowd, wanting to see if he could get closer to the front. As soon as he saw a man in red sitting on top of an elephant decked in jewels rounding the corner, he recognized what it was. It was the famous *Baraat* that he had read about when he first moved to India. The elephant passed by and the groom looked down at him, nodding ever so slightly. The crowd pressed forward, eagerly awaiting the sighting of the bride. Extravagant colors were everywhere. Suddenly, he felt someone pull on his arm and drag him into the parade. He didn't even see who it was as they had gotten lost in the shuffle. Soon he found himself dancing in the sea of colors and people.

Eventually, the celebration died down, but not before Colt had exhausted himself in the mayhem. He couldn't remember the last time he had danced. It had to have been when he was back in America, but it certainly hadn't been as much fun as that.

Per usual, Colt made camp along the shoreline. He had gotten used to sleeping under the stars. Since his life had consisted of so much upheaval, finding the constellations had been one of the only constants in his life, and seeing them brought him great joy.

The following morning as Colt made his way toward the harbor, he purchased a plate of *idyappam*—a steamed rice noodle dish. He had traded the rest of his precious sugar for it, but it was more than worth it. He enjoyed his breakfast, finding a spot that overlooked the Bay of Bengal. He eagerly watched the docks fill up with people, as he hoped to find a clue as to where he could find Deshi.

Colt didn't have to wait long before he knew he had found his man. A round, jolly fellow wearing something between a robe and a tunic with a white flowing beard marched right past him. The lively character entered into a paltry hut that was once a very vibrant yellow. It had since been discolored by the sun. A few minutes later, he opened what appeared to be a Dutch door. Colt assumed this meant he was now open for business. He walked up and peeked inside.

"Deshi?"

"Who's asking?" the animated man responded heartily.

"Darte told me to come and see you."

"Ahh, yes . . . Darte. I haven't seen him in years. How is he?"

"Good. He and his son are running the trading post together."

"Glad to hear that. His friends are my friends. How may I help you?"

"I need to get to Calcutta."

"There's an English charter that leaves around noon. I would be happy to make arrangements for you."

"I wanted to buy a sailboat."

Deshi sized him up. "Have you sailed before, son?"

"Not exactly."

"Then I don't think that would be the best idea. Sailing can be very dangerous."

"Nonsense." A strong British voice was suddenly heard from behind. "I would be more than happy to teach him. If we don't get it from you, we'll just go somewhere else."

Colt instantly recognized that voice. He turned around to see Peter who was smiling ear to ear. Colt was filled with confusion, joy, and guilt all at the same time.

"Uh, well, I might have something for you then," Deshi replied, equally confused as well by the Brit's appearance.

Colt tried to make sense of what was going on. But he was rebuffed.

"We'll talk after," Peter whispered. "Let's handle this first."

Deshi led them down the dock, passing by different boats. They walked to the very end toward a faded Bermuda sloop.

"I think this may be what you are looking for," Deshi said. "I call her the Queen Merry. She's not the prettiest, but she's dependable. I've had her for years, originally sailed her from Bombay when I first moved here. Before that, she was in Cape Town. She's never failed me."

Colt stepped into the 20-footer and gave it a quick inspection. He liked the size because it was clearly able to be operated by a single individual. Colt went down into the cabin. It was pretty tight, but he could definitely sleep down there, which is all he needed.

"She's perfect!" Colt said as he emerged back onto the deck.

Peter tossed Deshi a pouch filled with coins. "That should cover it. We are going to take her out for a test run." Deshi peered inside the pouch. He was perfectly happy with the contents inside.

"That'll be just fine, sir. Here, I'll get the line."

Peter stepped into the boat with Colt as Deshi untied the rope from the cleat.

"We'll be back."

"Take your time," Deshi said, tossing Peter the line and waving goodbye.

Colt couldn't contain himself any longer. He rushed over to Peter and hugged him, refusing to let go. "I'm so sorry. I shouldn't have said those horrible things."

"Colt," Peter said softly.

Peter could only get a word in before he was interrupted

by Colt: "I don't understand."

"Colt!" Peter grabbed him by the shoulders. "Listen to me, I forgive you. I know you didn't mean those things you said."

Colt sat down against the mast. The shock finally had caught up to him. "But what are you doing here? How did you know where I was?"

"Henri wrote to me immediately after you left Karaikal. He said that he had chosen to stay with his father, but that you were heading to Pondicherry to meet a man named Deshi. He also told me about the bizarre encounter with the witch. He told me everything. As soon as I got the letter, I went to the coast and took a charter here." Colt didn't say anything. He was still trying to process all of the information. "I've been here a few days, I'm just glad you finally showed up," Peter said, causing Colt to crack a smile.

"Wait. You aren't paying for this boat!"

"I planned on buying you the boat all along. That's the gift I wanted to give you a few weeks ago."

"But Peter!"

This time Peter interrupted him. "It's already been taken care of. I know that showing up on my doorstep all those years ago was one of the worst things that ever happened to you. But I want you to know it was one of the best things that has ever happened to me." Peter reached out his hand. "Come on, we've got a boat to sail."

TWENTY-FIVE

Peter tugged on the halyard and the jib raised. The sailboat inched forward gathering momentum as the large sail caught the tailwind. Peter called for Colt and showed him how to secure the line.

"The first thing to know about sailing," Peter instructed, "is to know where the wind is coming from. Imagine a giant clock in front of you. When the hands are between 10 and 2, it's a 'no-go.' But everything else is fair game. Remember the wind and the water are your friends, work with them. Don't make it harder than it has to be."

Peter demonstrated and then Colt took the tiller. Peter showed him how to maneuver as Colt quickly got the hang of it. After a few hours of getting the basic functions down, Colt felt comfortable enough to bring the boat back to the dock without any assistance.

"Well, how did it go?" Deshi asked.

"He's more than capable of operating her by himself," Peter responded proudly.

"Excellent," Deshi replied.

All of a sudden, loud shouting and the thumping of hooves could be heard in the distance. People scurried out of sight as a cavalry of soldiers appeared at the docks.

"Quick! Get inside!" Deshi commanded. Colt and Peter didn't question him as they ducked inside of the hut.

Twelve French soldiers approached Deshi. They were led by a fiery officer named Leon. "Bonjour. Je m'appelle Deshi. Are any of you in the market for a boat?" Deshi greeted the men.

"Our informant in Cuddalore has reported that a young EIC spy is on his way to Fort William. He may be holding some very important information that could greatly hurt our cause. He must be found immediately." Leon spouted.

"I haven't seen him," Deshi replied.

"Don't play dumb with us. We know you showed him a boat earlier this morning."

The soldiers drew their swords.

"Okay, okay." He said trying to calm them down.

"Tell us what you know."

"Yes, I saw him, but the other man ruined everything."

"Other man?" Leon questioned.

"There were two men. Right when the younger one was about to buy from me, an older gentlemen showed up and talked him out of it. He assumed I was overcharging and said they would be able to find a better deal in Madras."

"Then what happened?"

"They left." Deshi pointed to the Queen Merry. "That's the one they checked out. Would you like to go look at it?"

"There's no need for that. Who was the other man?"

"I haven't the slightest idea. But he definitely had a strong British accent. Once, I found out they were not interested in buying a boat, I had no time for them."

"Why did you lie to us?"

"What did you expect? You stormed onto my dock. Naturally, I was going to be defensive." Deshi said convincingly.

"Ok. When did they leave?"

"About an hour ago."

"Let's go. We can still catch them before nightfall." The soldiers rode off, and Colt and Peter emerged unseen.

Colt was elated. "Deshi, thank you! You saved our lives!"

"There's nothing more I hate on this earth than the French." Deshi spit as he said it. "Why are they after you?"

"Because someone thinks I'm something I'm not."

"Colt, there's no time," Peter urged.

"Wait, I have an idea," Deshi said. "Colt, stay inside of my hut until dark. When the coast is clear, I will come and take you to the boat."

"But what about Peter?" Colt asked.

"Colt, don't worry about me. I'll be fine. Just do exactly as Deshi says."

Peter gave Colt a final hug. "She's going to be there. I just know it. Have faith."

"Thank you for everything, Peter." Colt fought back the tears.

"No, son, thank you."

—⊃

As night set in, Deshi came back for Colt. They crept down the dock toward the sailboat. Colt got in quietly as Deshi untied the lines.

"Stay low," Deshi whispered. "Let the current take you out. Don't put up the sails until you are far away from the harbor. I hope you find what you are looking for."

Colt slipped into the cabin, and Deshi pushed the boat out to sea. The sailboat gently floated into the Bay of Bengal.

—⊃

Colt awakened to the bright shining sun on his face. He was finally in the clear. The French soldiers were long gone by now and relief washed over him. He couldn't believe that Sharat had alerted the French authorities to his whereabouts. He didn't know why the EIC—and now the French Army—cared about him? The target on his back grew by the day and it didn't make any sense. In his mind, he was no one of importance. That's how he felt anyway. However, he knew his father didn't think that because he would constantly remind him that he was "special" and that he "had a great destiny." Colt didn't understand how the enemy could somehow realize that, but he couldn't.

He pushed away the unanswerable questions and focused on the task ahead, sailing to Calcutta. There wasn't a single boat to be found in sight. The water was calm. A light breeze came off the coast and carried him along. There was a freedom to being on the open water and an excitement like never before came upon him. He felt purpose and he believed he was doing the right thing. Maybe this is what his father had felt when he left for Patna.

He was still amazed that Peter had come all the way to Pondicherry. He wouldn't have come if it hadn't had been for Henri. He had been wrong to condemn him, just like he had been wrong to accuse Peter. Henri had a chance for the first time in his life to live with his father. It would have been selfish to deny him of that opportunity. He was genuinely happy for his friend and gratitude filled his heart.

The sailing to Calcutta went relatively smoothly. Truthfully, it was the easiest something had come to him in years, and he welcomed it. He was tired of continually going against the grain. The ease was nice for a change. Colt dropped anchor, checked his compass, and studied his map. He was right on course.

TWENTY-SIX

August
Fort William

Colt had finally made it. It had been years since he had last been on the Hooghly River—under very different conditions, of course. Now he was on his own terms, but just being back on the muddy water conjured up disturbing flashbacks. Fort William was getting closer. He wanted to get a good look to see if anything had changed. It hadn't; it was still as cold and foreboding as ever.

As the harbor came into view, Colt observed something odd. Several cargo ships were being loaded with strange goods. He was too far away to see exactly what was happening, but something seemed out of place.

He tried to get a little closer without being noticed. As he approached the docks, he saw what the "goods" were. Men, women, and children in chains were being forced onto the ships. He felt sick. The East India Company was trafficking humans. He couldn't imagine what these innocent people were going through. A part of him told him to sail as far away as he could from this place. But if he left now, he knew regret would haunt him for the rest of his life.

He sailed a mile past the fort and anchored near the mangroves, away from any maritime activity. He waded to shore. His plan was to go into the city to see if he could gather any information on the whereabouts of his mother. He made his way into town as inconspicuously as he could.

Colt entered the open market and stopped for a second to scan the crowd. Strangers were everywhere and he felt helpless. He did something he hadn't done in years; he looked up and said a prayer asking for guidance. He didn't know what he was expecting. He didn't even know who he was looking for. Perhaps he was trying to find a friendly face, someone who might be willing to aid him in his search and offer up some type of useful information. But it was to no avail. Discouraged, he sat down by the edge of a fountain in the middle of the square.

Just when he was about to give up, he heard a loud voice twenty feet away. A British soldier was arguing with a young woman. The man grabbed her arm and muttered something to her, but Colt couldn't make out what was said. She nodded without making eye contact and made a selection of green onions and cabbage from a nearby produce stand. There was something familiar about her. Remembering Burdwan wasn't that far away, he realized it could possibly be Zara. Excitement began to creep in and he stood up to get a better look. She had a scarf over her head, but he recognized her face. It definitely was her!

Colt, clearly aware of the soldier's presence, discreetly walked over to where she was. He pretended to examine a head of lettuce. "Zara," he whispered.

She almost dropped the cabbage when she saw him. "Colt?"

"I know you are being watched. Is there somewhere else we can talk?"

"My brother is a farrier at the stables. Find him."

The soldier moved toward her.

"I have to go." She walked away without looking back.

Colt was completely floored; not only did he get to see Zara, but he had spoken with her! Then it was over as soon as it began. His mind attempted to connect the dots, but he realized he didn't have the answers. He had to find Rafa, and he knew the stables would be at Fort William. Being overly cautious, he looked around to see if anyone had suspected him before he walked away. There were so many people milling around that no one noticed him.

The stables were located directly behind the fort. He understood if Rafa was working in a place like this, it wouldn't have been his first choice. The sound of neighing could be heard, and he could see the open pastures used for grazing. Two guards were posted at the entrance leading to the stables, and Colt knew better than to try to sneak past them. So, he waited to see if at some point Rafa would leave. Sure enough, at sundown, his old friend exited. He looked worn down by life. Not wanting to cause a scene, Colt followed Rafa at a distance for a few blocks and allowed him to get well beyond the complex.

"Rafa!" Colt finally said, hoping not to startle him.

"What do you want from me?" Rafa asked with trepidation in his voice, unsure of who was speaking to him.

Colt caught up to him and, looking at him intently, said, "Rafa, it's me!"

"Colt!" exclaimed Rafa, giving his friend a bear hug. "I knew you would come back!"

Rafa glanced around.

"We are not safe out in the open. Follow me." Rafa led Colt through the dark streets and into a dingy apartment in the heart of the city.

The aroma of cardamom rising from the kitchen made Colt feel right at home. Rafa's parents' house in Burdwan used to smell this way.

"Mom, I have a huge surprise for you! Look who came to visit!" Rafa said taking his mother by the arm.

"Who?" Bindu replied. She felt around for Colt. He didn't understand why she was having so much trouble. He was right in front of her. Then the awful truth dawned on him; she was blind.

"It's me, Colt." He said, taking her hand.

"My Colt?" A huge smile came across her face and she

gave him a long hug. He was at a loss for words, knowing something terrible had happened.

"And this is my wife, Chella." Rafa said happily.

"You are married? Congratulations!" Again, Colt was shocked by the news.

"Thank you! It'll be a year next month."

They took their places around the table and Chella brought out chicken curry and placed it before them. As they started to eat, Colt was reminded of his mother. She used to make chicken curry for him all the time.

"I know you probably have a thousand questions," Rafa began. "So, I'll just cut right to it. Everything changed when the EIC took over Bengal after Buxar."

Colt was quiet, allowing Rafa the time he needed before sharing what was certain to be change for the worse. Rafa continued, "Our people couldn't afford the taxes that were being placed upon us. Eventually, the crops failed. We fought back, but we lost everything, including my father. We came here because I knew I could get a job working with horses."

Colt sat in silence. He didn't how to respond.

Rafa took Chella by the hand. "It's bad," he said, "but we have it better than most. Colt, I must ask . . . how did you find me?"

"Zara told me where you were."

As soon as Colt said her name, the ears in the room perked up, especially Bindu's.

"How were you able to see her?" Rafa exclaimed.

"I saw her for a second in the market before she was taken away."

"Colt," Rafa hesitated. "She works for the EIC now."

"Rafa, what the hell is going on?" Colt inquired as anger seethed through him.

"We used to have a stand in the market. My mother made tapestries and Zara would sell them. One of the soldiers took a liking to Zara and wanted to take her for himself. But when she refused to go, we lost the stand, and my mother was brutally beaten." His voice trailed off.

Colt shook his head in disbelief. He felt terrible for them. He got up from the table and embraced Bindu. "I'm so sorry."

"It's ok." She reassured him.

"No, it's not ok."

"I'm alright Colt. Zara is who I am concerned about."

"Colt, there's something you need to know. Rafa cleared his throat and continued, "in order to set an example, Zara was taken from us and has become the official property of the EIC."

Colt rubbed his eyes as if he was trying to wake up from a bad dream. He couldn't take anymore. "They must pay!" he shouted.

"They will." Bindu said softly.

"When?" He said exasperated.

"We may never see it dear one, but they will pay. Ultimately, good will triumph over evil."

Colt was instantly brought back to his childhood. She had used the same phrase back then. He was amazed by her fortitude. He didn't know how she could stay so positive after suffering such catastrophic loss. The room went quiet.

"Colt, our hearts were broken when we heard about what happened to you and your mother. What the EIC has done to so many lives is atrocious. There is absolutely no excuse for their malicious cruelty, and I meant what I said. They will pay for their crimes in this life or the next one." Bindu reached for Colt's hand. "But you have to listen to me, you must let go of your anger or it will destroy you." He began to pull away from her, but she tightened her grip. "I have been where you are and I have felt every emotion that you have felt.

"How did you overcome it?" His voice cracked as he spoke.

"I knew that if I stayed angry then I would only hurt those who really needed me, especially my new grandchild."

"Wait, Rafa . . . are you? I mean, is she?" Colt looked over at Chella.

"Yes, we're pregnant." Rafa interrupted him with a bright smile.

"Rafa, that's wonderful!"

"Thank you brother, if we never would have come to Calcutta, I never would have met Chella."

"Let's let these boys catch up." Bindu chimed in. "It's so good to see you Colt. Just remember, there are people who need you."

"Thank you Bindu."

"Hang in there," she said before being led into the kitchen by Chella.

"Have you heard anything more about my mother?" Colt asked Rafa.

"No. But Zara might know something."

"Well, I'm going to get my mom out of that place tomorrow."

"It might not be that simple."

"What do you mean?"

"What if she's still kept under lock and key?"

"Do you think I care about that?"

"Colt, you need a plan. You can't just storm in there."

"Why not? What would you do if your mom was taken from you, and you hadn't seen her in years?" His frustration level was rising again.

"Colt, hey, I'm here to help you. I hate what you've had to go through. But we need to talk to Zara. She will know what to do. Once we hear from her, we'll get answers. She knows you are here."

It had started to rain while Colt walked back to his boat. He was torn. On one hand, he was grateful to see Rafa's family. Their words brought comfort, encouragement, and hope. But on the other hand, he was beyond perturbed. The news about Zara and Bindu added a new layer of affliction. Thunder crashed and lightning flashed across the sky, and he urgently picked up his step. It started pouring by the time that he got back. The rain that pelted the boat sounded like gunshots. But he was safe, for now at least.

TWENTY-SEVEN

A couple of days had gone by, and there still hadn't been any word from Zara. Colt had diligently checked in with Rafa every night when he left the stables. Finally on the fifth day, He received good news. Zara was able to get away and was willing to meet him that night.

As Colt entered into Rafa's place, he saw Zara clearly for the first time. She sat at the table with her mother. She was more beautiful than he could even remember.

"I'm so sorry about everything that's happened." He said delicately.

"I hear you want my help," Zara said, ignoring his comment. There was a coldness to her voice he wasn't expecting.

"Only if you want to give it."

"What do I get out of it?"

"What do you want?"

"Freedom." That was something she had longed for, for years. "I'll bring your mother to you. But you have to take me far away from here."

"I will take you anywhere you want to go. I'm just happy to see you."

"Deal," she said as she avoided meeting his eyes.

"How is she?"

"She's alive. That is all I know."

Colt was beyond relieved. He had known that deep within his heart, but hearing Zara say it alleviated any lingering doubts.

"Does she know you?"

"I'm not sure." She said hesitantly. "Look, we don't have much time."

Using various utensils from the kitchen, Zara set up a model of Fort William, and she gave Colt directions.

"This is where I am. This is where she is." Zara pointed at each end. "Every Saturday evening, the guard posted outside my room leaves his post to smoke outside with a group of soldiers. When he leaves, I'll go and get her. We will sneak through the school which isn't far from the stables." She traced a line with her finger. "That'll lead us to the bay where you'll be waiting for us."

"When?"

"Tomorrow at midnight. Be ready with the boat."

"I'll be there." Colt took off the necklace that Nita had given to him and handed it to Zara.

"I have to be getting back." She said abruptly and walked out of the apartment.

Colt turned to Rafa. "What about you? Will you come with us?"

"This is my home now."

"You know where we will be if you change your mind."

TWENTY-EIGHT

The moonlight tried to shine through the night sky, but it had been apprehended by the clouds. Colt watched the battle all evening from the back of his boat, hoping the clouds would continue to prevail. Finally, it was time to begin the short voyage. He sailed the Queen Merry along the Hooghly until he found the perfect spot a stone's throw from the dock. He waited in the shadows, as a light rain started to fall.

As Zara made her final preparations, she heard rapping at the door. She threw her half- packed bag on the floor and removed the tiger necklace Colt had given her, replacing it with a string of pearls. She opened the door to find Thomas Webb standing there.

"Zara, I see you are wearing the necklace I gave you."

"Of course, Thomas," she said, taking a step back.

"I was wondering if you wanted to take a stroll with

me tonight through the gardens?" he said as he walked into the room.

"It just started raining."

"Come on. It would be an adventure. You like adventures, don't you?"

"I'm too tired. Maybe tomorrow night."

"Why?" He took another step inside, his eyes wandering around the room as though he were trying to locate something.

"The General would not be pleased," she retorted.

"Since when have you ever cared about what he's wanted?"

"Since the day I became his property."

"O, Zara, you forget so quickly. You belong to *us*. The EIC is one."

He admired several fine pieces of jewelry on her vanity: a dazzling diamond necklace, a ruby ring, topaz earrings, multiple gold bracelets.

"Do you remember the days when you had nothing? You were a poor girl in the marketplace, struggling to make ends meet. Now look at you. You are the envy of every woman in the northeast."

"You destroyed my life."

"I saved you."

"You know what you did to me."

"I thought you enjoyed it." He said, moving closer to her. I sure did. It was one of the best nights of my life." Webb stroked her hair gently. "You know I care for you Zara. I always have. Look at everything I've done for you. Carnac wouldn't even know you existed if it wasn't for me."

Webb picked up two of the gold bracelets and put them on her wrists. "You know what the problem is?" Webb stated. "The General doesn't know what he has."

"What do you want, Thomas?"

"Isn't that obvious?" He moved closer. "He sees you as a slave. But to me, you are so much more. Imagine what we could do together, the things we could accomplish. I could be emperor and you would be my queen. It would be just like the days of Babur. Your people would flourish once again."

"Why are you saying all of this now?"

"I knew if I stayed silent, I would lose you forever."

"Lose me?"

"Zara, why do you play me for a fool?" He walked past her and lifted up the bag stuffed with clothes. "What is this?" he demanded.

"Old clothes from my mom. I haven't been able to unpack yet."

Taking her by the neck, he squeezed as hard as he could. "Don't lie to me!" He let go of her and she dropped to the floor gasping for air. He straightened his jacket and composed himself. "Do not lie to me. Who is he?"

"Who?" she screeched.

Webb grabbed her again and forcefully threw her onto the bed. "I will ask you one more time and I better have an answer I like, or else your brother will never meet his new child. Do you understand me?"

Zara slowly nodded her head.

"Now, who is the man who just pulled alongside of

our dock twenty-five minutes ago?"

"He is a Dutch trader."

"Thank you. Now that wasn't so hard. What does he want from you?"

"Nothing." She stopped, understanding the power of her own words. "He doesn't want anything from me." She stared pensively out of the window.

"I don't buy it. All men want something. I know exactly what he wants. The lonely Dutchman has fallen for the beautiful Zara and in return you get what? A life at sea? Give me a break, you would hate that. You've gotten a taste for luxury. Nothing less would satisfy you." He played with the rich pearls along her neckline.

"He promised freedom."

"There's no such thing. We are all slaves to something."

"He was different."

"We are all the same," he scoffed. "Come. Let's take care of this once and for all."

She hesitated for a second but took his hand, and they walked out of the room together.

TWENTY-NINE

Colt could see two figures approaching. Euphoria set in and he quickly pulled the anchor up. Tying the line loosely, he climbed up onto the planks in anticipation. It was still too dark to see clearly. One of the silhouettes stopped moving and the other ran toward him. The footsteps became louder, and Zara came into view.

"I'm sorry, Colt," she breathed, incredibly upset.

"Hey, what's the matter?"

"You have to leave."

He threw his arms around her. "Talk to me," he said tenderly as he held her for a brief moment.

"Get away from me!" she shrieked and pushed him away. Thomas Webb walked forward out of the shadows and into the moonlight. The rain began to fall harder now.

"I will handle this, darling," Webb said to a completely astonished Colt. "You have no business here. She isn't leaving."

"What will she cost?"

Webb put his arm around Zara. "She's not for sale."

"Well, I'm not leaving without her. You can bring her down here or I will go up and get her myself."

"Who do you think you are?" Webb glowered.

"I'm Colton James D..." Zara turned to Webb and passionately kissed him, preventing him from finishing his sentence.

Webb pushed Zara away. "Listen here, Colton James. I don't know who you are. Nor do I care."

"Come on, let's go back upstairs." Zara grabbed Webb's hand, wanting to lead him away.

"There will be plenty of time for that."

"Zara, w-w-what are you doing?" Colt stammered.

"I don't have time for this." Webb whistled loudly and six soldiers at his beck and call marched onto the dock with torches. He pointed at Colt, and they viciously attacked him beating him mercilessly.

"Zara!" Colt cried out.

The soldiers hit him again and again as Colt tried to evade them. But they were too much for him and he was finally pinned to the ground.

"Zara!" Colt cried out once more.

Webb kicked Colt in the face, knocking him completely out. "Leave no trace," Webb said as he stepped over Colt's body and away from the pool of blood forming on the dock. "And when you are finished, clean up this mess."

Webb looked to Zara, "Let's be going, dear."

Zara took one last look at Colt before taking Webb's

outstretched hand. She knew what would be coming next and could hardly stomach the thought. With her heart broken in pieces, she followed Webb to his quarters.

The moon ducked behind the clouds as the soldiers dragged Colt's lifeless body across the dock, leaving a trail of blood on the wooden boards. They lit the sails on fire and hurled him into the sailboat. After untying the line, the soldiers pushed the boat out to sea. The flames rose higher up the mast and engulfed it. Catching the current, the Queen Merry floated idly toward the Bay of Bengal, looking like a funeral pyre raging against the black night.

THIRTY

The heavens let loose, and the deluge was underway as the weather turned treacherous. The winds howled and the water level on the Hooghly rose higher and higher while the sailboat was being thrashed by the waves. The sails, once on fire, were extinguished by the rain. But they were in such poor shape that they were nothing but tattered rags, hanging from a severely damaged mast. The sailboat floated for hours downstream as Colt lay on the deck, unconscious.

As he finally began to come to, Colt was confused to see water pouring onto him. He couldn't remember where he was; all he knew was that he was in a lot of pain, especially his head. He touched his face, and his hands were covered in blood. He then remembered the events that had just taken place. Something crashed above him and the boat bobbed up and down. He listened intently and heard another loud crack. The mast had finally given way.

Knowing he didn't have much more time, he willed himself onto his feet. Fighting through the pain, he went down into the cabin to grab the leather satchel. He tried to bail out as much water as he could, but it was too late. Soon she would capsize. Colt heard one final crack before he jumped into the river.

The process of submersion had begun. Now it was just a matter of time before the Queen Merry would be totally underwater. As she went down, a few chunks of wood had broken apart and floated to the top of the water. Colt grabbed the largest piece and held on as the rain continued to beat down upon him. He looked for any sign of land, but the fog prevented him from seeing anything. Using the broken board as a raft, he climbed onto it; he didn't want his dangling feet to attract a crocodile. Holding on, he continued to float downstream as he waited for daylight.

THIRTY-ONE

The Island
Some 50 miles away from Fort William

Dawn finally approached as the longest night of Colt's life ended. The wind had subsided, but the sun was nowhere to be found. The fog blanketed everything before his eyes. He couldn't tell where the sea stopped and where the sky began, but at least it was getting lighter. He floated for a while longer until he saw a dark mass before him. He knew it had to be land. He waited until he got a clearer view. Once he was certain, he gingerly swam the rest of the way, protecting his ribs as best he could.

Once he made it onto the sand, he collapsed from exhaustion. The sun peaked through the clouds and the fog lifted. Aside from the pain in his face and ribs, his hands had cuts all over them and his shoulder was badly bruised. His stomach growled, but he didn't have the energy to move. As reality of his situation sank in, despair soon followed. He closed his eyes and wished for death.

Chirp, chirp, chirp. A small wood sandpiper flew next to him.

"Go away," Colt groaned at the bird, throwing a handful of sand at him.

The bird chirped even louder causing Colt to sit up.

"What do you want?"

The bird continued to chirp at him. He stood up. Now he was talking to animals; he was sure he wasn't the only one to ever to do that on a deserted island.

"Fine, are you happy?"

The bird chirped one more time in a cheerful tone, implying he was indeed happy before flying away. Colt was not impressed. He examined his new surroundings. He wished he had his maps and compass, but they had gone down with the ship. Nevertheless, he remembered at the edge of the Hooghly before the Bay of Bengal, there were a cluster of islands. He concluded he had to be on one of those.

He rummaged through his sack, looking to see what had made it through the storm. He laid all of his possessions out on the sand. There was a machete, a rope, a sweater, soaking wet paper, a quill, a glass inkwell, a Bible, and two small pouches—one filled with a few coins and the other with lentil seeds. His stomach growled once more. He popped a seed into his mouth and slowly ate it. As he was about to put a second one in, he abruptly stopped, realizing he may need these. Horrified, he put the seeds back into their pouch. He looked over his things again, this time noticing his father's Bible. He could feel the animosity toward the old book rising within him. He ran to the water and launched it forward with all his might. As soon as he let go, he grimaced in pain. He had completely forgotten about his aching body. The Bible disappeared beneath the waves. He picked up his machete furiously and walked away from the surf directly to a wooded area in search of food.

He discovered the island formed a near perfect circle and he came back two hours later with a half dozen coconuts. Colt cut into the coconuts, finding just enough meat to tide him over but not enough to fill him up. However, it was better than nothing and his thirst was finally quenched. He needed to create some type of shelter. This problem was solved when he found some giant palm leaves. His machete came in handy for this task. He stacked the leaves on top of each other and formed two rows facing one another about three feet high. Then he placed the largest leaf over the top which served as a makeshift roof. He set his belongings inside, passing out next to them. He woke up in the middle of the night to more raging winds. His temporary dwelling was torn apart. He wriggled underneath of what was left.

The night finally passed and it wasn't long until he heard the sound of chirping again. His friend was back, chipper as ever. The little bird hopped toward Colt and warbled at him.

"I have nothing for you," Colt groused.

The bird chirped at him again. Rising out of the mess of leaves, Colt foraged for an old coconut.

"Here." He tossed the bird a small piece of meat he had been able to shake out of it. The bird gobbled it up and flew away.

"You're welcome!" Colt shouted after the bird. He headed to the palms to find breakfast. The sun was finally out, and the wind had faded into a gentle breeze.

As he approached a tree with about a dozen coconuts hanging high above, Colt got out his machete. He hacked at the trunk, hoping that his force would knock a few of them down. The tree didn't budge. He swung a little bit harder. Still nothing happened. He swung as hard as he could and his machete stuck in the tree, and not a single coconut fell down. He dropped to the base of the trunk and cried out at the top of his lungs.

"What do you want from me? What did I do to deserve this?" Colt screamed.

With his hands raised to the sky he screamed louder. "Answer me! What did I do wrong?"

Nothing but silence ensued.

"Please! I'm begging you," Colt pleaded as he fell on his side and sobbed. He couldn't take anymore. His body heaved up and down in the gritty sand. Dust, sweat, and tears clung to his face.

After fifteen minutes of lying there, he heard something. He looked up to see a coconut in the process of falling to the sand. It thudded softly beside him. He picked it up, stared at it, and then flung it away from him. He cursed at the top of his lungs. It was too late.

Darkness had overtaken him and he knew what he must do. He hurried back to camp to grab the old rope. Once he had it, he sprinted back to the trees. He was now in hot pursuit of the spot where he would take his last breath, and he couldn't wait to get there.

Not far from where his machete had lodged into the tree was another palm leaning heavily toward the water. He had climbed it the day before, taking off every coconut he could find. He crawled up the tree for the second time. When he was about twelve feet off the ground, he tied a knot around the trunk. He used the other end to tie the noose. He put the noose around his neck and tightened it. The tree was sturdy and he had secured the rope as best as he could. He was seconds away from freedom now. All of his pain would be gone. He took one last breath, closed his eyes and jumped.

THIRTY-TWO

What happened next was a blur. As soon as the rope was lengthened, it snapped and Colt fell straight to the earth, landing awkwardly on his ankle. Pain shot through his body as he stared up at the rope which now dangled above him. He loosened the remaining rope from his neck only to find the problem—the rope was so waterlogged it couldn't support him. He slid it off and tried to stand up, but his left ankle was in so much pain that he couldn't put any pressure on it. His ankle was black and blue and the size of a grapefruit. Exhausted, he again looked up at the sky. Only this time, he said nothing.

The months passed and Colt's ankle slowly healed, as did the rest of his body. He had made the island as comfortable as he could. He finally pried his machete from the tree, and with it he managed to create a stronger and more fortified hut. He made a fire near his new home out of sticks and dry leaves. Every so often, the sandpiper would visit him—the little bird that used to bother him now brought him great joy. Aside from finding crabs, he caught fish using a homemade trap made from woven palm leaves. He lived on these along with a staple diet of coconuts.

As he worked on a new net one afternoon, the idea of planting the lentils came to him. He hadn't thought about the tiny seeds since the day that he landed. He decided to go for it, curious to see whether or not they would take root. He had close to thirty seeds. He dug four trenches and put the seeds into rows in the center of the island. Sure enough, not long after, green shoots appeared. He checked on them every day, and little by little they continued to grow. Three and a half months went by, and he had his first harvest. He was very pleased. Instead of keeping the majority of what he had reaped, he only kept about fifteen percent and planted the rest. He planned on doing this over and over again.

One evening as he sat around his campsite, he retrieved the paper and inkwell from the hut. He dipped his quill in the ink and began to write.

Peter,
I don't know if you will ever read these words.

But it makes me feel better to think that one day you will. I'm sure you are wondering what's happened to me since I last saw you. It's not really a story I want to re-live at the moment. Let's just say things didn't go as planned. In fact, they went opposite of how I imagined they would go. I then attempted to do something I'm terribly ashamed of.

All I will say is, someone kept me alive that day. Someone kept me alive for a reason. Someone that I've hated; someone I've blamed for everything bad that has ever happened to me when in all reality, it wasn't His fault. I finally realized that as I stared at the sky from the flat of my back, more hopeless than I had ever been before. On that day, my life changed forever. I understand now that we are all tiny pieces of an extraordinary puzzle—a puzzle that will never fully make sense until all of the pieces have been put into place.

As I sit here underneath the stars, reflecting over everything that has happened to me. I can't help but to believe I'm where I'm supposed to be. I know my father's death was not in vain. Meeting you and everyone else on my journey wasn't just a random coincidence. I was destined to come to this place. I know that my story is not over. For the first time ever, I have a deep peace within my soul.
Colt

THIRTY-THREE

September 1773

Colt walked back from the water with several *ilish* he had caught in his newest trap. He proudly showed the fish off to the little bird that had recently flown in to check out the latest catch.

"Sahil, we got a few more today," Colt said, as he tossed a fish to the bird. The little bird chirped while another sandpiper flew in.

"I see Nisha is back, you've been with her a lot recently."

The bird chirped at him.

"I'm not being nosy. I'm just stating a fact."

Both birds chirped at him.

"Okay, okay, I'm sorry. I won't bring it up."

As the two birds enjoyed their lunch, Colt went to

check on his lentils, which by this point had taken over almost the entire island. The four rows he had started with had turned into over four hundred. The island had become a full-blown lentil farm. It certainly wasn't his intention, but he had become so preoccupied with caring for the tender plants that it had become his passion. Every day he walked the rows, making sure each and every plant had exactly what it needed to grow. They grew very well in the tropical climate. There weren't any animals that bothered the plants and being so near to the river, the plants always had enough freshwater. A few times Colt debated on leaving his oasis, but whenever he would think about the tiny plants, he decided to stay.

As Colt was getting ready for bed after another long day, a northeast wind picked up. Not thinking too much about it, he drifted off to sleep. He was soon awakened by loud crashes of thunder accompanied with bright lighting that lit up the night sky. The wind was deafening. He hadn't experienced a storm like this since the night he first got to the island. He could feel his home starting to come apart, but there was nothing he could about it.

At first light, he emerged from what was left of his shack and surveyed the damage. Broken branches and leaves were everywhere. He ran to see if his plants had made it. Miraculously, they had survived! The outer layer of trees had blocked the wind from doing any harm to the interior of the island. All that had been destroyed was his hut.

As he returned to his campsite, Sahil flew in and started chirping at him.

"That might have been the worst storm I've ever seen here," Colt said, as he started to collect debris. As the bird flew away, Colt called out: "Thanks for the help."

As Colt continued to clean up, the bird returned and chirped very excitedly.

"What is it?" Colt asked.

The bird flew toward the water and circled the sky. He looked over at Sahil when suddenly, he saw something. A rectangular object was lying on the sand by the shoreline. Colt went over to see what it was. It was his father's Bible. It had washed up during the storm. Colt couldn't believe it! He picked it up. It was soaked, but surprisingly enough, it wasn't in too bad of shape. As he flipped through, his eyes fell onto the first page with his grandfather's writing:

John,
Congratulations on the birth of your son! I hope that he will make you as proud as you have made me. Let this book be your guiding light, it will never steer you wrong.
Love,
Dad

Colt had never opened it before. He clutched the Bible tightly to his chest and for the first time in his life, he cried from a place of joy.

As he sat there simply amazed, he heard Sahil chirping again very loudly. Colt could see that the bird was circling something again. Colt laid the Bible to dry out at the camp site and jogged over to see what the bird wanted to show him. Lo and behold, a giant palm tree was lying on its side and coconuts were all over the ground. It was the same tree where he had almost made the biggest mistake of his life.

"It was struck by lightning," Colt surmised, as he rubbed his hands over the charred wood. An idea began to form, but he refused to let his mind go there.

Over the next few days, Colt continued his daily routine on the island, but he could not stop thinking about his wild idea: turning the tree into a canoe and sailing it back to Fort William. No matter how many times he dismissed it, he couldn't shake the desire. He had to at least try. He realized he wasn't meant to stay here forever. He knew the island was a place where he could heal from the past and prepare for the future. His enemy had sent him away thinking he had destroyed him. But what was intended to be his prison had become his liberation. He wrestled with it for another two days, but he couldn't deny what he felt any longer. The Bible itself was a sign. The more he read it, the more hope it gave him. A storm had brought him to the island and a storm would take him away from it.

Before he would even try to cut it, he had to fix his dull machete blade. Finding a rock near the water's edge, Colt sharpened the blade with painstaking precision. With his new sharp edge, he cut off the remaining parts of the tree that were connected to the roots. With dogged determination, he dragged the heavy trunk through the sand back to his camp.

The following day he began the actual construction

of the dugout. His goal was to make it close to twelve feet in length and a little less than three feet in width. Weeks passed, and the tree slowly morphed into a canoe. Using a trick he had once read about, he lit the inside of the trunk on fire in order to hollow it out. It worked perfectly and after the majority of the wood had been burnt away, he carefully manicured the edges making the inside as smooth as he possibly could. Using the machete, which was sharpened daily, he shaped the boat until he was completely satisfied. Using the wood that was left, he carved out a paddle. His project had been completed and the time had come for him to test the canoe.

He pushed the boat into the water. Just as he was about to climb into it, he stopped. He stared at his creation as anxiety gripped him. Paralyzed by fear, he couldn't bring himself to get in. Instinctively, he took his machete from his side and struck the canoe. He did it again and again, leaving a deep gash in the perfectly shaped wood as tears rolled down his cheeks. If he continued, he would do serious damage. He flung his machete onto the sand as sobs came from deep within him. The monster that had been locked inside of him had finally broken free.

"I can't! I can't!" he cried aloud.

What he had initially wanted so badly, he didn't know if he wanted anymore. This place had become his safe haven and he didn't know if he was ready to leave it. He preferred the captivity of comfort over the glory only freedom could bring. If he tried to obtain that freedom, that would mean he would be forced to pay a price he might be unable to pay. When he had attempted something like this before, he had failed miserably. Who was to say this would be any different? Before he came to the island, his life had been filled with heartache and loss. But on the island, he was sheltered from the pain of the world. He was safe here. He had everything he needed. No one bothered him and his heart could not be broken. He brought the canoe back onto land and went to his favorite place on the island.

THIRTY-FOUR

Surrounded by little green plants, as he watched the sun dip out of sight, Colt was reminded of Zara. A faint smile flashed across his face. He missed her more than words could express. He had once been in a field like this with her after the sun had set many years ago. It was the night he found out his father would be leaving for Patna. He remembered the conversation as if it were yesterday and replayed it over in his mind, just as he had many times before.

"He's leaving," Colt had said as he cried into her shoulder.

"I'm so sorry, Colt," Zara had said as she wrapped her arms around him and rested her head on the top of his. They had held each other tightly, neither wanting the moment to end.

"I don't know what I'd do if something happened

to him."

"Colt, listen to me." Just hearing her voice had brought him comfort as he gazed into her soft brown eyes.

"I don't understood why things happen the way they do, especially the harder things in life. But one thing I am sure of is you."

"Me?"

"Yes!" She had stood up animated. "I wish you could see what I see when I look at you. I've never met anyone who has more passion or perseverance than you. It doesn't matter how many times the odds are stacked against you. You always find a way to pull through. This time won't be any difference."

"Do you really think so?"

"I know so," Zara had said as she sat back down beside him and kissed him on the cheek.

Colt snapped back to reality. The woman he last saw was definitely not the girl he used to know. But deep down he knew how much he loved her and always would. If he ever saw her again, he would still take her wherever she wanted to go.

His mother's face now came to his mind. She was the one who had suffered the most. She was the one who had been kept against her will. While he was in school and doing all the things he had done over the years, his mother had been confined in that awful place. Every night, she probably wondered how long she would have to be there. He didn't know how many nights she had cried herself to sleep. If he chose to stay on the island, she could potentially remain in Fort William for the rest of her life. He considered the orphans from St. John's and the humans the EIC were trafficking. How many more would have to suffer? Righteous anger emanated through him.

If you don't, who will?

He finally heard the voice that his father had always talked about. With new resolve, he stood up and dusted himself off. He would put the canoe into the water and head to Fort William. And whatever was supposed to happen would happen. He would relinquish his right to be in control. As wonderful as his time had been in this special place, it was time to leave.

⬯

Colt's canoe was laden down with lentils and coconuts. He took one last look at the island and pushed the boat into the Hooghly with fervor. As he dipped his paddle into the sea, he heard two birds chirp as they flew toward him. They landed on the shore a few feet from him.

"I was hoping I would see you both one more time," Colt exclaimed.

The birds chirped at him.

"I'm going to miss you too."

The little birds flew along the shoreline as the canoe faded from sight.

THIRTY-FIVE

December
Fort William

Colt could tell something wasn't right. For one, it occurred to him that he hadn't seen a single ship on the river during his entire trip. The second sign was that the farmland that used to be lush and green was now barren and brown. He made his way toward the shore, wanting to get a closer look. He could see gallows in the background. He hardly saw anyone outside except a lone fisherman on an empty dock.

"What's happened here?" Colt asked from his canoe.

"Where have you been?"

"South."

"Famine. Set in four years ago. Devastated everything."

He took a moment as he allowed it all to sink in. He was stunned by what he had just heard and couldn't find the right words to say. He could only imagine how many lives would have been taken as well. He didn't know whether to feel guilty or grateful, seeing he could have easily been one of the ones who hadn't made it.

As he continued along, he couldn't help but to notice the shallow graves and the stench of rotting corpses. His heart broke for the people of India and what they had been through. Millions of lives had been lost because of the East India Company. The EIC didn't control the weather, but he understood they had played a major role in the destruction. It wouldn't be long, he hoped, until justice would be served.

He could see Fort William now. The once busy port had become a ghost town and he paddled right up to the dock. He was calm and relaxed as he stepped onto the wooden planks. He tied his canoe up and walked across the dead grass, his machete hanging from his side. Colt approached the wide-open gates which at one time were so grand and prestigious; now they were anything but that. The number of guards that had once guarded the menacing fort had been cut in half. The few on duty appeared unimposing and apathetic.

Colt walked right through the gates. No one bothered to pay any attention to him. His long bushy beard made him almost unrecognizable. As he entered the courtyard, his eyes darted around for the best way to the get to the back of the complex. He soon found a route that went through what appeared to be a flower garden. This was the first sign of real plant life he had seen since he left the island. Passing by purple irises and yellow poppies, he stopped suddenly. On a patio inside of the garden, General Carnac and Thomas Webb talked amongst themselves. They were sipping tea in high-backed chairs, without a care in the world. Knowing this was his chance, Colt stealthily crept toward them undetected. He slipped right behind Carnac's chair and held the machete to his throat.

"Remember me?" he whispered.

Webb stood up from across the table and pointed his pistol at Colt.

"Guards!" Webb shouted as four EIC soldiers came running over with rifles.

"Pull that trigger and he loses his head," Colt answered back without blinking an eye.

"Who is this?" Carnac gasped, feeling the blade at his neck.

"It looks like my old friend Colton James has risen from the dead," Webb said.

"My name is Colton James Door. You murdered my father, and now I've come back for my mother."

"Door?" Webb was confused.

"Yes, yes," said Carnac, terrified. "Take whoever and whatever you want, just please let me go, I beg of you."

"Where is she?"

"Who?" Carnac pleaded.

"My mother. Annie Door."

"She's in the schoolroom," Carnac said, and then to the guards: "Go get Miss Annie now and bring her here."

Two guards ran off as they followed Carnac's order.

How long has it been since I've last seen you?" Carnac enquired.

"Ten years, two months, eleven days." Colt breathed.

"Has it been that long? Well, let me have a look at you, boy!"

"You don't need to see anything."

Carnac tried to twist out of Colt's grasp, but Colt pushed the blade deeper into his neck as red drops of blood fell onto his crisp white shirt.

Carnac slumped back into his chair.

"Just say the word, sir, and I'll take care of him right now." Webb pulled the hammer back and placed his finger on the trigger.

"Put the gun down, Thomas. We cannot afford to have any more of London's inquisitions."

Thomas reluctantly put the gun down.

"Bring my mother to the harbor. The General and I are going for a walk."

Colt seized Carnac and forced him to stand up. Carnac walked out to the courtyard with Colt in horror. By now, dozens of soldiers had been alerted of the precarious situation. They pointed their guns at Colt, not knowing what to do. The razor-sharp blade was ready to strike at any moment. Colt marched past all of them with a steely gaze focused solely on making it through the gates.

They passed through and onto the street which was now starting to fill up with citizens of Calcutta. It seemed word had gotten out that General Carnac had been taken captive. The people of the city wanted to see the show unfolding before their very eyes. Colt released the blade but kept a firm grip on Carnac's collar. Feeling the release of the machete, Carnac noticed the crowd that had formed and pleaded with the people.

"Help me. Help me. He's a mad man. Will somebody help me?"

The Bengalis did nothing.

"One thousand rupees to whoever kills him. Ten thousand!"

There was no response.

"Do you know who I am?"

The people still didn't move.

The water wasn't far way away now. Colt turned to face the fort when he caught a glimpse of his mother. He tried to hide his emotion.

"When she's down here, I want your men back inside of the fort with the gates locked." Colt whispered into Carnac's ear, the blade once again putting tension on his skin.

The streets were completely filled now as all eyes were on Colt and General Carnac. Annie moved closer to the harbor. When she looked up to see Colt, her eyes widened, and a smile broke out on her face as they locked eyes.

"Bring her to me," Colt demanded.

Hubert and Lawrence, the soldiers who Colt remembered from years before, did nothing. They just stood there, holding onto Annie tightly.

"Bring her forward, you idiots!" Carnac's voice was shrill and filled with fear. Hubert and Lawrence brought her forward.

169

"Give the order," demanded Colt as he dug the blade in deeper.

"Get inside of the Fort and lock the gates behind you," Carnac screamed.

Hubert and Lawrence were stunned, along with the dozens of soldiers who stood by watching the drama unfold.

"Get back inside. That's an order!" Carnac pleaded. The soldiers reluctantly walked away leaving Colt with his mother and General Carnac.

"Don't ever come near my family again," Colt threatened. "Do you hear me?"

Carnac nodded very slowly. Colt took his mother by the hand and released him, who sprinted into the crowd of people, trying to get away from Colt's machete as quickly as possible.

"I knew you'd come," Annie said, as tears of joy streamed down her face. Colt put his arm around his mother as they walked directly to the dock passing by hundreds of beaming faces. The canoe was in sight. Freedom was closer than ever before.

All of a sudden, a gunshot went off, and Colt fell to the ground. A hush fell over the crowd as Thomas Webb emerged with his pistol raised.

"Did you think you would just get away?" Webb laughed, as he twirled the gun in his hand. Colt lay there, blood oozing from the bullet hole in his back.

"No one takes from the EIC and gets away with it." Webb addressed the crowd. "Let this be a lesson to all of you."

Webb moved toward Colt and was about to fire off another shot. He lifted the pistol when—out of nowhere—a shovel hit him over the back of the head. He dropped to the ground, and Zara hit him again. Her heroic deed stirred the people who ran to the entrance of Fort William. They broke down the gates and entered the courtyard.

Annie cradled Colt's head. "Colt! Colt, stay with me. Help! Someone get a doctor," she pleaded.

I just wanted to see your face one more time," Colt said weakly as he clasped his mother's hand. He went in and out of consciousness. Two men hurried over, picked Colt up, and carried him to a nearby house where a doctor laid him on a table.

THIRTY-SIX

Three days later

Colt blinked his eyes several times as he adjusted to his new surroundings. He could see water outside of his window as the curtains swayed back and forth from the gentle breeze.

"Good morning, sweetheart!"

"Mom?"

She knelt beside his bed. "I'm right here."

"I tried to get here sooner."

"*Shhh*," Annie whispered.

Colt attempted to lift himself out of the bed.

"I have to see Rafa."

"There will be time for that, just rest." She gently pushed him back down.

"But he has to know," Colt said before he fell back into a deep sleep.

Colt woke up hours later to see Rafa sitting by his bedside.

"Rafa," Colt barely managed to say.

"Colt, you won't believe what's happened. The people have gained control of Fort William! Carnac and Webb are going to be tried for war crimes!"

"It's over?"

"Yes, it's all over. The EIC is bankrupt, and Hastings is bringing sweeping reforms."

"Hastings?"

"He is the new governor general. He's not that great, but he's better than Clive or Carnac."

Despite all the pain, Colt was overcome with joy. He could hardly believe the news. As he tried to sit up, he saw the child in Rafa's arms.

"Your son!" Realizing he was unable to lift himself, Colt slid back down on the bed.

"His name is John Rafa," Rafa said proudly. "We will talk more. Right now, you need to rest. Keep taking the medicine the doctor is giving you."

"Take my canoe fifty miles south."

"What?"

"There's so much food." Hearing the conversation from outside of the room, Annie walked in briskly with Bindu. "Bindu, please listen to me. Tell Rafa he has to harvest the crops." Colt uttered softly, his eyes beginning to droop.

"Colt, all of the crops failed." Rafa asserted.

"Not mine."

"Rafa, I think you need to listen to him." Bindu advised.

"He's been hallucinating," Annie said as she rested her palm on Colt's forehead, checking his temperature. "He keeps talking about an island and someone named Sahil." Rafa took Colt's hand. "Get some sleep. We'll be here when you wake up."

Colt gripped his hand tighter and opened his eyes. "Rafa. Take my canoe. Follow the river southeast as far as you can. Trust me." Colt slipped back into a comatose-like sleep before he could say anything else.

Having no clue what Colt was talking about, Rafa left the room puzzled. He thought that all of the crops had been destroyed by the famine. Leaving his son with Chella, he went down to the docks where he could see Colt's canoe tied up. As he got closer to the dugout, sure enough along with Colt's leather bag, the canoe was filled with produce.

⟜ͻ

Rafa paddled furiously toward Fort William. Once more, the canoe was laden down with coconuts and lentils. What he was able to take with him was nothing compared to what had been left on the island. He knew this wouldn't erase the devastation of what had happened during the famine, but it would feed some, and it would—more importantly—bring hope. He concluded that as soon as he returned, he would find a much larger boat and take as many people as he could back to the island. There was so much more to be harvested.

～ɔ

Zara rocked back and forth in anguish as she knelt down beside Colt's bed. "I'm so sorry, I'm so sorry," she muttered repeatedly under her breath.
Colt opened his eyes to see her.
"You're supposed to be sleeping," she said.
"I didn't know if I would ever see you again,"
"I didn't know if you would ever want to see me again."
"I'm really glad you are here."
"I was so scared. I didn't know what to do," she said ashamed, unable to meet his gaze.
"Zara," Colt said, and her eyes slowly met his. "Everything is how it should be." He took her hand, their fingers interlocking. He slowly sat up on the bed, shifting slightly to make room for her. She climbed up beside him and placed her head on his shoulder. He kissed the top of her head, "I'll still take you wherever you want to go."

～ɔ

A week later, two little birds fed their young as they

watched dozens of people harvest the lentil fields. The Bengalis laughed with joy as they filled their baskets, knowing better days were ahead for Calcutta as well as all of India.

EPILOGUE

June 1776
Harleysville, Pennsylvania
8,000 miles away from Fort William

The bright orange sun had just dipped below the horizon as an elderly gentleman helped his wife up from her rocking chair. Apart from the cloudless sky, nothing seemed out of the ordinary. However, just when he was about to go inside, something caught his eye. It looked like someone was on his property. Stepping away from the door, he tried to get a better look. He soon saw that it wasn't just one person, but three people were walking toward the farmhouse. All he could tell from their silhouettes was that the trio consisted of a young married couple and a middle-aged woman. As they got closer, he could see the younger woman had darker skin and was clearly pregnant. Then suddenly, he recognized a smile he hadn't seen in a long time. It was Colt's.

AFTERWORD

◊ It is estimated that ten million people died in the Great Bengal Famine of 1770.

◊ Founding Father, John Dickinson, in one of his famous letters called "A Letter from the Country, to a Gentleman in Philadelphia" warned the early colonists that the East India Company would try to "repair their broken fortunes, by the ruin of American Freedom and Liberty." He was concerned that what had happened in India could easily happen in America. His warnings were heeded, and not long after he wrote his letter, the colonists threw over 90,000 pounds of EIC tea into the Boston Harbor.

◊ Robert Clive was tried before Parliament as the British government investigated the operations of the

East India Company. He was eventually acquitted of all charges. But in 1774, he died from a fatal wound to the throat by his own hand from a penknife. No suicide note was written, and his death is still shrouded in mystery.

◊ John Carnac was dismissed from the EIC and passed away in Mangalore in 1800.

◊ In 1857, a revolt took place among the sepoys against the EIC. As a result, the British government stepped in, and the EIC was formally dissolved in 1873.

◊ India finally gained independence from Great Britain on August 15, 1947.

◊ Fort William is now the headquarters of the Indian Army's Eastern Command.

◊ St. Johns Vestry Anglo-Indian Higher Secondary School is still in operation today.

GLOSSARY

Avial- A South Indian delicacy made of vegetables cooked with spices and coconut oil

Baraat- An Indian wedding tradition where the groom travels to the wedding venue which is often the bride's home

Chapati- A type of flat bread that is very popular in India

Chettinad Chicken- A spicy, savory dish with red chilies that is from Tamil Nadu

Chital- A spotted deer that is native to the Indian subcontinent

Dayan- An evil and powerful witch in Indian folklore

Dholes- A wild dog found in Asia

Diwali- The Festival of Lights and India's most important holiday

Diya- An oil lamp used during the celebration of Diwali

Emperor Fish- A popular fish among Indians that are

found in shallow reefs

Gaur- Also known as the Indian bison and is the largest species among wild cattle

Ghee- Pure butterfat that is very similar to clarified butter

Hookah- Water pipes used for smoking tobacco

Idiyappam- A steamed noodle dish made from rice flour

Ilish- The state fish of West Bengal that's also known as a hilsa

Keerai Kootu- A traditional South Indian dish made from spinach, lentils, and coconut

Kite- A bird of prey that is from the same family as hawks and eagles

Marwari Horse- Rare breed with unique curved ears that served as warhorses for the Rajputs

Mavirar- A Tamil word used for Warrior or Hero

Mutton Biryani- The most popular dish in all of India which consists of meat, onions, and spices mixed with rice

Nawab- A ruler in India during the Mughal Empire

Rangoli- An art decoration often used to celebrate Diwali

Rupees- currency used in India

Sahib- An Indian word used for "sir" or "master"

Sambar Deer- The largest deer in Asia

Sari- A traditional woman's garment that originated in India

Sepoy- An Indian soldier who served the East India Company

Sundal- A South Indian dish that consists of stir-fried chickpeas and curry leaves

ACKNOWLEDGMENTS

I just wanted to take a moment to say that I really appreciate you taking the time to read my book. There are countless ones to choose from and the fact that you chose to read mine means the world.

In the spring of 2019, I drove to Santa Barbara with my mom and I shared with her an idea for a movie that I hoped to make one day. Little did I know that that conversation would be the beginning of *The Crown Jewel*. As the years passed, I began to take notes and write down additional ideas. Then in 2020 when the pandemic hit, I lost my job temporarily and I finally had the time to write. I locked myself in my room and I typed up the first draft of my script on my old trusty HP with Microsoft Word 2007. After I finished, I showed it to my parents and my dad recommended that I turn it into a book. So a few months later, I left my job for good and wrote the novel.

Writing a book is not an easy task and I did not get here by myself. I had an incredible team around me who helped me cross the finish line. I want to thank my relatives Sam and Anita Price for allowing me to write this book in their beautiful home in Jamestown, NY. They were beyond gracious and provided me with everything I needed. I would frequently drive around Chautauqua Lake and receive inspiration from the picturesque scenery. It was truly the perfect place to write.

I want to thank my editor Nicole Hayes at JH Writing. She graciously fixed my mistakes and gave me such insightful feedback. During the editing process we had a long conversation and she provided me with a crucial critique that really helped me iron out some major details. Thanks again Nicole!

I would also like to thank my book designer Rose Newland of AIA Publishing. She did a tremendous job on the cover and formatted the entire book. Rose lives in Australia and was such a pleasure to work with. Rose, you are truly amazing!

Thank you to the "University of Texas Libraries" for allowing me to use the 1760 map of India.

I have saved the best for last, my parents. Thanks Mom and Dad for all that you have done for me throughout the years. There is no way this book would have been written without your love, support, and most importantly your encouragement. Not many parents would encourage their kids to leave their homes and jobs to follow their dreams and passions, but you did. Even when times got tough, you always stuck by my side. You are truly one of a kind and it's an honor to dedicate this book to you.

Throughout the majority of my life, I have always been surrounded by people from India and I really hope this book honored them and their culture. What their ancestors went through was unimaginable. Growing up in the West, I had never heard anything about this period in history. When I finally heard this story, I knew it must be told. The United States of America as we know it wouldn't exist without the suffering that took place in India as well as many other places in the world.

Tyranny is a terrible thing and we must never let history repeat itself.

Milton Keynes UK
Ingram Content Group UK Ltd.
UKHW040933180224
437992UK00012B/319/J

9 798989 666577